# The Additional Investigations of

# Sherlock Holmes

## Arthur Hall

### Edited by David Marcum

Paperback ISBN 978-1-78705-973-3

ePub ISBN 978-1-78705-974-0

PDF ISBN 978-1-78705-975-7

MX Publishing

335 Princess Park Manor, Royal Drive,

London, N11 3GX

www.mxpublishing.com

Cover design by Brian Belanger

Arthur Hall was born in Aston, Birmingham, UK, in 1944. His interest in writing began during his schooldays and served as a growing ambition to become an author.

Years later, his first novel 'Sole Contact' was an espionage story about an ultra-secret government department known as 'Sector Three' and has been followed, to date, by five sequels.

Other works include six 'rediscovered' cases from the files of Sherlock Holmes, two collections of short stories featuring The Great Detective, two collections of bizarre tales and two novels about an adventurer called 'Bernard Kramer', as well as several contributions to the ongoing anthology, 'The MX Book of New Sherlock Holmes Stories'.

His only ambition, apart from being published more widely, is to attend the premier of a film based on one of his novels, ideally at The Odeon, Leicester Square.

He lives in the West Midlands, United Kingdom, where he often walks other people's dogs as he attempts to formulate new plots.

His work can be seen at: arthurhallsbooksite.blogspot.com, and the author can be contacted at: arthurhall7777@aol.co.uk

By the same author:

*The 'Sector Three' series:*

Sole Contact

A Faint and Distant Threat

The Final Strategy

The Plain Face of Truth

A Certain Way to Death

The Suicide Chase


*The 'Bernard Kramer' series:*

The Sagittarius Ring

Controlled Descent


*Volumes of fantastic short stories:*

Facets of Fantasy

Curious Tales


*Rediscovered cases from the files of Sherlock Holmes*:

The Demon of the Dusk

The One Hundred per Cent Society

The Secret Assassin

The Phantom Killer

In Pursuit of the Dead

The Justice Master

Further Little-Known Cases of Sherlock Holmes

Tales From the Annals of Sherlock Holmes

Contents:

The Adventure of the Disappearing Prisoner

An unseasonably fine March morning can hardly be anything but pleasant, yet I felt that the day had begun strangely. To my surprise, I discovered my friend Mr Sherlock Holmes in high spirits at breakfast, a state of affairs so unusual that I felt compelled to remark upon it.

"I would think from your pleasant expression, Holmes, that you have solved the Merriton bank fraud case that Lestrade was so concerned about."

He looked up as I took the chair at the opposite side of the table. "Indeed, I was at last able to obtain the evidence that I have been seeking since the arrests. Hoffnan and his group had no defence against it, and will doubtlessly spend the remainder of their active years in prison."

As I began my breakfast he proceeded to relate the details of the succession of deductions which had led to such a satisfactory conclusion. These I would record at the first opportunity, for possible future publication. I finished the last of my toast and drank my coffee, before rising and moving to the window feeling Holmes' eyes upon on me. I looked out into Baker Street to see that the early spring sky was still an unclouded blue. A cold but bright sun shone down as passers-by huddled into their thick coats, wearing mufflers and gloves.

"Yes, Watson," he said, as if had read my thoughts. "It is indeed a beautiful day for the time of year and, to anticipate your question, I would be amenable to a brisk walk in Hyde Park or St James Park or anywhere else that appeals to you. I have no new case to distract me at the moment, although I await the results of several enquiries. So, what do you say, old fellow, shall we take the air for an hour or so?"

But it was not to be. We had left our lodgings behind by no more than fifty paces, when a police coach swerved to the kerb ahead of us.

"It is Lestrade," Holmes observed at once. "I very much regret that our walk is likely to be postponed."

The little detective fairly dashed from the coach, coming to rest breathlessly as he accosted Holmes and myself.

"Good morning, gentlemen," he began. "I regret this intrusion but I thought you would like to hear what I have to say, Mr Holmes, especially as you helped the Yard to put Cutter behind bars."

"Cutter?" Holmes retorted. "Ephraim Cutter?"

"He is to hang at the end of the week," I recalled.

"Indeed he was, Doctor," Lestrade confirmed. "But he disappeared from his cell in Pentonville, during the early hours of this morning."

Holmes gave the Scotland Yard man an incredulous look. "Come now, Lestrade. What sort of foolishness is this? Men cannot pass through solid walls, and I would wager that there are few more solid than those of a condemned cell. Have you visited Pentonville and examined the walls and surroundings? There is surely some trickery here and I cannot say I am surprised – Cutter showed himself to be an imaginative and cunning adversary during the investigation."

Lestrade nodded his bulldog-like head. "Very true, Mr Holmes, and I have seldom encountered a man who deserved his fate more. At the Yard, we have discovered six victims, at the last count. His method never varied. He would kidnap the child of a wealthy family, extract money from them and then return to them a strangled body. I believe he considered this safer than leaving alive a child who could possibly identify him."

"I am familiar with the case, inspector. I conclude from your avoidance of my question that you have not yet visited the prison. How then, did this notion of a miraculous escape come to be?"

"We will discover that when we meet the Reverend Arnold Chester, the prison chaplain. That is of course, if you gentlemen will consent to accompany me."

He indicated the coach and Holmes glanced at me. I nodded my assent because, although I was disappointed at the postponement of our walk, I found myself intrigued by Lestrade's narrative.

Little was said, during the journey. Holmes sat with his head upon his chest and the inspector wore a distant look – doubtlessly wondering as to the outcome of this strange situation. As for me, I had been this way with Holmes before, and as we entered Barnsbury my past impressions of the drab confines of the prison returned to my mind.

The coach came to a halt and Inspector Lestrade approached the gate to speak to the guard within. After a moment we were admitted, to be met by a heavily-built man of perhaps forty years.

"Good morning, gentlemen," he said as we alighted. "We were advised of your coming. My name is Gramwell. I am Head Guard of the condemned cell block and the governor has instructed me to accompany you there and to provide any information or assistance you may need."

Lestrade acknowledged the man and requested him to lead us to Cutter's cell, whereupon we were taken to a small building that was set apart from the main structure. On entering I felt again the claustrophobic and depressed feeling that I remembered from my previous visit. The inspector too appeared uncomfortable as he regarded the stone walls and tiny cells which had been the last residence of many evil souls. Only Holmes seemed unaffected.

Gramwell led us around a corner into a short corridor and stopped abruptly. A thin and nervous-looking uniformed guard stood talking to a man wearing the dark clothes of a priest, outside a cell with its door wide open.

"Gentlemen, allow me to introduce you to the Reverend Arnold Chester, our prison chaplain, and Andrew Bellows, who had special responsibility for the condemned man, Ephraim Cutter." Gramwell's disapproving tone made it clear that he blamed Bellows for Cutter's disappearance, although how this could be when the nature of this strange event was as yet unknown was difficult to comprehend.

Lestrade introduced Holmes and myself, before Gramwell announced that he would leave us to conduct our interviews unimpeded, but would be close at hand if needed.

There was silence for a moment, during which Holmes' gaze took in the dull surroundings before returning to the two men before him. The Reverend Chester was the first to speak.

"Mr Holmes, I confess to being confounded by all this. Mr Cutter's conversion was remarkable, a true miracle, but I could not have imagined that he was to be taken literally."

My friend regarded him thoughtfully. "I am as yet unfamiliar with the recent situation here. Pray relate, in your own words, what has occurred."

"I visited Mr Cutter soon after his arrival at Pentonville." The priest averted his eyes, as if he found the memory an embarrassment. "I found him to be an evil man, given to curses and blasphemy. He boasted of his crimes and showed no remorse. During subsequent visits however, I noticed a gradual change. The man's resistance softened. He began to listen when I quoted the Bible about God's arrangement for atonement and forgiveness, and a new hope dawned in his eyes when I explained that to Him no man is beyond redemption."

"Could this have been a subterfuge?" I asked.

"With what object? I was convinced of his sincerity simply because his fate was sealed. He was about to face the hangman, nothing could change that. He would gain nothing by pretence."

"He would be far from the first to undergo such a change, with the prospect of approaching death," Holmes observed. "Did his new-found faith increase, in response to your instruction?"

"Very much so, in fact he began to tell me of visions that he had begun to experience as he slept. This went on for several weeks, until he revealed to me that he believed God was about to set him free. I explained to him that he must not take this to mean that he would be released. The message, if indeed it was genuine, surely meant that forgiveness for his crimes was possible. This did not satisfy him, and on one occasion he shouted his belief that he was soon to regain his freedom so loudly and adamantly that the guards had to be called to quieten him."

Holmes looked up sharply. "When did this occur?"

"The evening before last. He kept repeating that God was about to come for him."

"And then, a little more than one day later, he disappeared from his cell?"

5

"So it would appear," the reverend shook his head. "I have never heard or experienced such an event. Frankly, I do not know what to believe."

A faint smile crossed Holmes' features. "We shall see what is revealed by looking into the matter." He turned to Lestrade. "Have you any questions for the Reverend, Inspector?"

Lestrade, who had remained silent until now, looked mildly uncomfortable. "Not as yet, Mr Holmes."

"Then perhaps we can continue with whatever Mr Bellows can tell us."

The guard who had been assigned especially to watch Cutter, possibly to prevent him from cheating the hangman by ending his own life, shrank visibly. "I can tell you nothing that I have not already explained to Mr Gramwell, and the governor," he stammered. "I began my duty, the early shift, and found this cell empty. There was no sign of the prisoner, nor any indication as to where he might have gone."

"Do you believe that he was removed by the hand of God?"

Bellows looked at the stone-flagged floor uncertainly. "I could not say, sir. The prisoner once told me that he expected the Almighty to come for him in a blaze of glory."

Holmes nodded, slowly. "And do you see any sign that this has occurred?"

"None, sir."

My friend walked around the cell. "Not even these substantial burn marks on the floor here, and on the lower walls? Come now, Bellows, you must have noticed these despite the poor visibility in here, and having done so must have formed some sort of explanation. Why, I can still smell traces of smoke in the air."

Lestrade peered into the semi-darkness. "I see them, Mr Holmes, but cannot understand how there could have been fire, without kindling."

"Perhaps, then, it was God's work," said Bellows.

Holmes moistened a finger with saliva and brushed it across the discoloured stonework. It came away coated with a deep crimson hue.

"Not unless our Creator announces Himself with a blaze of permanganate of potash, mixed with a little glycerine. The effect of that combination is much like a miniature volcano, with much fire and smoke. I am surprised that the fire brigade was not summoned at once." He paused, I thought for effect. "But of course, as Cutter was the only occupant of the condemned block, no one else would have noticed. Except for you, Bellows. What have you to say to that?"

The guard could maintain the deception no longer.

"I had to do it sirs, they have my family. The prisoner Cutter said that my wife would be found floating in the Thames and my children would be returned to me hacked to pieces over the next few weeks. I did not want to betray the trust that had been placed in me, but what else could I do?"

"Most of Cutter's gang escaped the police net because there was no evidence against them," Holmes recalled. "Some were his relatives. They would have been easily capable of organising such a scheme to set him free. I do not doubt that they would have carried out their threat or indeed, may yet do so." He turned to the weeping guard. "Have your family been returned to you, Bellows?"

His answer was a distraught shake of the head.

"So, we have disproved any divine intervention in this matter. Now we must ascertain how Cutter left the prison. How did you assist him?"

The young man sat in a corner of the cell with his head in his hands. He looked up at us with shamed and fearful eyes. "I gave him my spare uniform."

Holmes nodded. "Are the guards and visitors required to sign out when they leave the premises?"

"They are required to sign both in and out as necessary."

"Pray find Mr Gramwell in the corridor, and request him to bring the attendance ledger here. Tell him it is of the utmost importance that I examine it."

Bellows left quickly and without a word. He returned within ten minutes with a large leather-bound volume.

"Mr Gramwell apologises for the delay, but he had to obtain the governor's permission."

"Very well." Holmes took the ledger and ran his finger along the entries for the early shift change-over. "How many guards work in this part of the prison?"

"There are five of us, to accommodate the various meal breaks and reliefs."

Lestrade and I peered over Holmes' shoulder, as he identified every entry. "As I expected, over the course of an hour or so six men signed out. Again, there is no mystery regarding Cutter's exit."

"I will have every constable in London on the lookout for him." Lestrade assured us.

"A wise move, inspector, but it occurs to me that I may be able to narrow down his likely whereabouts on consulting my index. Watson and I will now return to Baker Street, and you no doubt will be anxious to get back to the Yard." He fixed his gaze on the wretched form of Bellows, who was still visibly shaking and pale. "As for you, there can be no doubt that you are guilty of a serious dereliction of duty. Nevertheless, I cannot find it in myself to condemn you entirely." I saw a look of surprise enter Lestrade's face at this. "Because I have asked myself how I would have acted in your place and found no different answer, I will intercede on your behalf with the prison governor. I cannot say what your fate will be, but I will endeavour to reduce the harshness of it. I am certain that Reverend Chester also will assist with this."

The priest assented, placing an arm around Bellows' shoulders as we left. In the corridor we confronted Gramwell who was eager to learn what had transpired. Holmes evasively told him that all would be explained when we returned, probably the following day, for a meeting with the governor. He asked the head guard to arrange an appointment and confirm this by telegraph to Baker Street. The man looked taken aback at this, but nodded his assent when Lestrade voiced his agreement.

"Do not assume yet, that the hangman will not be needed at the appointed time," were Holmes' parting words to the dismayed head guard.

The police coach delivered us back to our lodgings. As we alighted, Holmes informed the inspector that he would communicate with him by telegraph the moment he was able to confirm his suspicions. "A glance through my index should suffice, Lestrade. I cannot quite recall the date, but I am certain that Cutter's likely whereabouts were mentioned in an article

9

published in *The Standard*. On receipt of my message, your attendance in the company of, say, six armed constables would be as well. I recall that his associates, including his immediate family, are in every way as villainous as he, though nothing as yet has been proven against them."

The inspector nodded. "In addition, I will ensure that every man on the beat is aware that Cutter is again at large."

The official vehicle rattled off and Holmes and I were back in our rooms in minutes. Mrs Hudson appeared to inform us that the luncheon hour had approached, only to be waved away by my friend who was on his knees racing through page after page of his index. I, being fully conscious of increasing hunger pangs, gratefully accepted a portion of veal and ham pie and the stewed apple that followed.

I had hardly put down my coffee cup, when Holmes stood up with a triumphant shout.

"I have it, Watson! I have it!

"You have discovered Cutter's hiding-place?"

"I am certain of it, sufficiently so to inform Lestrade. A recent newspaper cutting mentions, here in the small print, that Cutter's sister and her husband are the owners of the steam launch *Erica*, moored in the Port of London near Tower Bridge. I would wager that Cutter has taken refuge there."

"Would they not have sailed by now?" I ventured.

"I would have expected so, but perhaps the tides were against it, or it was necessary to gather supplies for what is undoubtedly intended to be a long voyage. At any rate, there is no mention of such a departure in the sailing lists of any newspaper. I imagine their intention is to conceal themselves among the network of

English rivers until they feel that police interest in them is waning. By then, Cutter will have had sufficient time to change his appearance as he has done before."

The glitter in Holmes' eyes meant, I knew of old, that the game was again afoot. I handed him his hat and coat and hurriedly put on my own, and we stood in Baker Street awaiting a cab moments later. We interrupted our journey to the Port of London but once, for him to vanish into a Post Office to send the promised telegram to Lestrade. Soon the sinister shape of The Tower was evident, before we left the hansom near the bridge. We descended and walked cautiously along a narrow footpath, noting the name of each tethered vessel as we passed. The river curved slightly, and we saw on the opposite bank several open barges which appeared to be deserted. A number of dormant steam launches rode the water unsteadily, disturbed by the wake of a craft heaped with coal. I saw that for a good two hundred yards ahead nothing else was berthed.

"There!" Holmes exclaimed suddenly, indicating a half-rusted tub moored near a group of overhanging trees. "I can just make out the name of the vessel. It is the *Erica*."

"She appears to be deserted."

"Which is precisely what Cutter would have us believe, is it not, until an opportune time to set sail arrives. Are you armed, Watson?"

"My hand rests upon my service weapon."

"Excellent. I also am prepared. We have no means of knowing how many opponents are concealed in there, so I think we will await Lestrade and his men before making an approach. It would be best to avoid any shooting if that is possible, for to the best of our knowledge the wife and children of our friend Mr Bellows remain captive. Let us hope they have not been harmed,

11

or that the *Erica* does not leave her berth within the next half-hour."

We stood in the shadow of a tall stack of crates, listening to the movement of the Thames and the passing of its shipping, but never once averting our eyes from the *Erica*, before we heard the heavy tread of the approach of the official force.

Lestrade demonstrated uncharacteristic caution in keeping his men concealed, for they remained some way off as he responded to Holmes' signal and joined us.

"You discovered their hiding-place quickly, Mr Holmes."

"A quick search of my index was all that was necessary. I knew I had seen a reference to Cutter or his family, quite recently."

The little detective nodded. "According to our files at the Yard, Cutter alone has been convicted of a crime, although most members of his family have been suspected of robbery at one time or another. Unless the others break the law today, he is the only one we can arrest."

Holmes looked at Lestrade and beamed. "Inspector, I was considering a number of approaches to accomplish this, whilst preserving Bellows' family unharmed. I do believe that you have just supplied the answer I was searching for. If we are successful, you will truly deserve all credit for the outcome."

Lestrade's expression was blank, and I saw that he had not understood my friend any more than I had myself. We waited for Holmes to disclose his plan.

"Inspector," he said at length. "I would be obliged if you would order your men to form a line along the bank, in full view of the *Erica*. I assume that every man is armed?"

"All six constables have been issued firearms, Mr Holmes, as you requested in your message."

"Capital! If you will leave it to me to converse with Cutter, I believe I can resolve the situation."

Lestrade was silent for a moment, and appeared as puzzled as before, but he did not dispute Holmes' intentions. "Very well, Mr Holmes."

We remained in concealment while the constables took up their positions. They stood in a line near the wide wooden plank that bridged the gap between the shore and the *Erica*'s deck. Each man brandished his weapon, presenting a formidable barrier to escape.

Without a word, Holmes strode out to stand where he was easily visible from the boat. After watching the vessel for a short time, he cupped his hands to his mouth and hailed those within.

"Halloa, the *Erica*. Ephraim Cutter, you are hopelessly outnumbered. Surrender yourself now, and much bloodshed can be avoided."

The faint echo of his words died away, without any discernible effect.

I believe he was preparing to repeat his message when the cabin door was slammed open violently. Two men stood on the threshold. I recognised Cutter from his trial, which I had attended with Holmes, but his companion was unknown to me.

"Jake Quintly," Lestrade said, anticipating my question. "A cousin of Cutter, not known to be on good terms with him, usually. He's slipped through our fingers many times because he intimidates witnesses, but his day will come."

"I'm sure it will," I replied, observing the large bearded man with a long scar above his left eye.

Even from this distance I could see the blank stare, that of the wild beast, that Cutter had invariably worn in the courtroom. He reached behind him, into the shadows of the cabin doorway, and dragged forth a young woman who cried piteously as he placed her in front of him with his arm about her neck.

"See here, Mr Sherlock Holmes and all you coppers," he cried in a hoarse voice. "if you try to stop this boat from leaving here you'll all be sorry. I'll slit this tart's throat and then both her brats, and you'll see them float down the river behind us. What do you say to that?"

As his words died away I heard sounds from some of the constables that indicated their horror and revulsion. Even they, accustomed as they were to the dark aspects of life in the capital, were affected by the pitiless cruelty of this man. Never more, I told myself, was a man more justly condemned.

"That would be foolish in the extreme don't you think, Cutter?" Holmes replied after a moment. "It cannot have escaped your notice that Mrs Bellows and her children are the shield that prevents these officers from opening fire. Kill them, and what protection for you remains?"

Cutter hesitated, and Quintly gave him an uncertain look.

"We have guns too. We'll take some of you with us. I will never face the hangman."

"That may be, that is how it could turn out. But how many of your family are in there? How many will die needlessly in the battle?" Holmes paused to let Quintly, not Cutter if his intention was as I suspected, take this in. "I must tell you that you alone are wanted by the law. Inspector Lestrade assures me that none of your family have ever been convicted. This means that, provided Mrs Bellows and her children are returned to us unharmed, all that is required for them to sail away unmolested is your return to custody."

In the short silenced that followed, I saw Quintly's expression harden. I remembered that Lestrade had mentioned that the two were rarely on friendly terms, despite their family connection. Cutter turned to Quintly and spoke quickly, apparently voicing a curse or oath, before they retreated back into the cabin with Mrs Bellows who sobbed loudly.

"I don't think you've convinced him, Mr Holmes," said the inspector. "You can't appeal to the better nature of a man like Cutter. If nothing happens within the next ten minutes, I'll give the order to open fire."

"Lestrade!" I protested. "Remember the woman and children in there."

"It is not my choice nor my wish, Doctor, but I am under orders not to let Cutter escape. How many more children might die, if he is allowed to resume his activities?"

"Let us be patient, while they consider the situation," said Holmes. But the words were hardly out of his mouth when the cabin door was flung open again momentarily and Mrs Bellows and a small boy and girl pushed roughly onto the deck. At a sign from Lestrade, one of the constables laid down his weapon and stepped aboard the *Erica* to assist them onto the bank. They were hurriedly removed from the scene as sounds and cries of much violence erupted from within the vessel. We looked on as the door opened for a final time, and a bruised and bloody Cutter staggered onto the deck. At once the constables' guns were raised, but there was no need. Cutter appeared ready to make his escape in the river but Holmes, seeing that he was unarmed, boarded the boat with a

15

single leap and restrained his adversary with the grip of steel that I had seen him apply before. Both men had regained the bank and Lestrade fastened police handcuffs on Cutter's wrists, before a man I had not seen before appeared in the wheelhouse and a heavily-built woman freed the line. Clouds of steam appeared as the engines burst into life, and the craft shuddered. The vessel left the bank slowly, then more quickly as the current took her and swept her out of our sight.

"We have, I think, won the day on this occasion," Holmes observed.

The little detective walked back along the bank with us. "Mrs Bellows and her children are safe, Cutter will probably hang as was arranged previously, Mr Holmes. But the others on that boat could have been charged with kidnapping and assisting a convicted escaped prisoner. I cannot help but feel little satisfaction, for we have achieved only a partial victory."

"I concur of course, Lestrade," Holmes said a little disappointedly, "but on occasion one has to take the view that in life, by its very nature, things often do not turn out exactly as we would have them. As it is, you will undoubtedly have further opportunities to apprehend other members of Cutter's family for future misdeeds, and I have already stated that full credit for this encounter is justly to be yours. As for the immediate future, I suggest that you instruct your men to convey Cutter to Scotland Yard, to await your arrival after you have shared the excellent dinner that I know Mrs Hudson has prepared for us at Baker Street."

The Adventure of the Drewhampton Poisoner

In response to repeated requests from my publisher, I have recently approached my friend Mr Sherlock Holmes on several occasions, to enquire whether any of our past cases that have been hitherto withheld for one reason or another, could now be laid open to public scrutiny. His reply was not at first favourable, nor was it enthusiastic, for he has always maintained that our exploits should be viewed as exercises in logic and reasoning, rather than as tales of the dramatic and mysterious.

At length, and with the utmost reluctance, he gave his permission. This was more, I have not the slightest doubt, to ensure that I would press him no further, than for any desire for fame or notoriety. I believe that I have mentioned the following events in passing, and only once in my writings until now. To my surprise I find that my notes are incomplete, and so I must rely on my ailing memory to assist in relating this affair to the public to the best of my recollection.

March had been a month of very mixed weather. Two weeks of intermittent storms were now succeeded by days of warm weather that suggested a pleasant spring ahead. Holmes' mood had been deteriorating for some time despite his recent successes, as it always did when he was starved, as he put it, of mental stimulation.

On one such morning, Holmes and I had left the breakfast table and were about to settle ourselves in our armchairs to enjoy our first pipes of the day, he collecting yesterday's dottles from the mantleshelf, when I chanced to glance through our half-open window to look down upon Baker Street.

"Holmes!" I called to him, and he looked towards me in response. "Unless I am much mistaken, you are about to acquire a new client. There is a fellow running towards our door as if the devil were after him, dodging in and out of the passing traffic."

His expression lightened immediately. "If he is indeed intending to visit us, let us hope he has something interesting to offer. You may have noticed, Watson, that I have not been my most amiable self, of late."

"Not at all, dear fellow," I replied with a tactful, if not completely truthful, assurance. "Ah, it seems I was right."

The door-bell rang loudly and we heard Mrs Hudson answer almost immediately. There followed some momentary discussion, during which I formed the opinion that our landlady was enquiring whether the caller had secured an appointment. His voice rose at this, betraying the conceived urgency of whatever had brought him to our door, whereupon Mrs Hudson allowed him to enter and preceded him on the stairs.

Holmes answered her knock with a bid to enter, and a tall man, ashen-faced and trembling, was shown in. We rose from our chairs as our landlady withdrew, for it was clear that our visitor was far from well.

"My dear fellow, come and rest yourself in this basket chair," my friend said concernedly.

I put an arm around our new client's shoulder and guided him. He shivered violently under my touch and his expression was of someone deeply troubled.

Holmes quickly poured a measure of brandy from the decanter, and the man accepted it gratefully. When he had drunk much of it he set the glass down on a side-table, beside the top hat which he had removed before entering.

"Are you feeling any improvement?" I asked him.

"Thank you, yes. I am most grateful to you gentlemen," he replied in a stilted voice. "Recently this strange condition has come upon me. Our local physician can make nothing of it, other than to say that it may be stomach cramps and to prescribe a powder, but I have formed my own conclusions. It is poison you see, the cause of the deaths of several in our village, but I know not from whence it comes."

"And this is what has brought you to us?" Holmes enquired.

Our visitor glanced from my friend to me, and back again, looking confused.

"You are Mr Sherlock Holmes?" he ventured.

"Indeed I am, and this is Doctor John Watson before whom you may speak as you would to me. When you are feeling better, pray take a moment to consider all that you have to tell us and begin at the beginning without omitting the slightest detail. Be assured that we will do all that we can to help you."

The man began to breathe more steadily, and drained his glass before pausing to collect himself.

"I am Mr Ahab Rampling," he began in his unsteady voice. "I hold the position of farm manager on the estate of Sir Trevill Bertram, near the village of Drewhampton, which is not far from the Surrey border. Recently a plague has descended upon our village, or at least that is what most folk there believe, but I am certain that there is evil afoot. I am quite sure that someone, for reasons I cannot imagine, has in some way introduced a substance that continues to claim the lives of some of the villagers. I believe also that this is the cause of my present state."

Holmes had been listening intently, with his fingers steepled beneath his chin.

"Have the victims been both men and women," he asked.

"They have. Two men and two women have died."

A few moments passed and both Mr Rampling and I glanced towards the window, attracted by the curses of a cab driver whose anger was apparently directed at someone obstructing the passage of his vehicle.

"Have you made your suspicions known to the local force?"

Our client smiled painfully, as if the suggestion was ludicrous. "The nearest police station of any size is in Guildford, more than forty miles away. Constable Jessop, who serves our village and works out of tiny premises with a single cell, is as puzzled as everyone else. Until now, you see, the most serious crime that has ever taken place there was when Albert Crawley allowed his horse to gallop down the high street and frighten the children outside the school."

"An admirable record," Holmes acknowledged. "But tell me. Sir, is there anyone who you, yourself, suspect as the cause of these unfortunate deaths?"

Mr Rampling endured a fit of coughing, for which he apologised profusely, before replying. "I confess that there is not. However there is an unfounded opinion among the villagers that the landowner, Sir Trevill Bertram, is to blame. He is a rather bohemian figure, and it is believed, I understand, that he visits a witch after dark, to obtain substances and spells."

"But what possible reason would he have? I presume the victims are among his tenants?"

"Some of them are, sir, and the story has no sense to it. That is why I am here, Mr Holmes, to clear Sir Trevill's name in the eyes of our village."

Holmes lapsed into a silence that lasted so long that Mr Rampling, like many before him, looked to me to confirm that my friend's attention was still with us. I made a reassuring gesture and our client nodded.

"Mr Rampling, do you know of any person in your village who has travelled abroad, particularly to the tropics in, let us say, the past year?" Holmes asked suddenly.

Our client shook his head. "I am certain that there is no one. Such an absence would have been considered an unusual event, and certainly remembered."

"As I would have expected." Holmes turned to me. "In view of the prevailing warm weather, I think a trip to Surrey would be rather pleasant, Watson, if you would care to accompany me."

I assented at once, of course.

"It may be a day or two, I regret we are unable to visit your no doubt charming village sooner, but we will certainly look into this." Holmes rose and, seeing that the interview was at an end, our client did likewise. "And so, we will bid you good-day, Mr Rampling. We trust your health will be much improved when we see you in Drewhampton."

#

Mrs Hudson happened to be on the stairs wielding a brush and dustpan, and so Holmes and I were left undisturbed as she assumed the task of showing our client out.

My friend's expression had deepened and he appeared asleep or lost in thought for several minutes, before his eyes opened and he shifted his thin frame in his chair.

"We can, of course, immediately discount any involvement with witchcraft or wizardry," he murmured, "although I would like to know, given these circumstances, what association Sir Trevill Bertram has with such supposed practices."

"What then, could be the cause of these deaths?" I asked him. "Mr Rampling's symptoms, such as I was able to see, could be indications of anything from a failing heart to a fever."

Holmes turned to me with a glint in his eyes. "Oh, I believe our client to be quite correct, Watson, this is almost certainly a case involving poison of some sort. The mystery here is the identity of the perpetrator and, of course, why he is conducting this apparent vendetta against the village."

"That is why you asked Mr Rampling whether anyone local had recently travelled abroad – you suspected that any such person might have brought back some exotic and deadly herb?"

"Precisely, but I will form a more accurate impression when we arrive in Drewhampton. As it is, I delayed bringing my attention to this affair because it suddenly struck me that I am now in a position to bring to a close a case I undertook some months ago which appeared to have no motive or solution." He rose from his chair and wandered to the window, and I saw his posture alter as he looked down into the busy street. "In addition, I see that our friend Inspector Lestrade has just emerged from a hansom and is walking briskly to our door. Doubtlessly he has need of our help, so it is as well that we did not promise our services to Mr Rampling immediately."

As it was, the inspector's request took up an unexpected amount of Holmes' time. It was, in fact, fully four days before we found ourselves alighting from a local train which set us down in Drewhampton after a short journey.

"How unfortunate," he remarked as we emerged from the station into a short and tree-lined lane, "that we were unable to procure a trap or cart. Ah, but perhaps such a conveyance is unnecessary, since I see that the outskirts of the village begin at the end of this avenue of elms. Do you see, Watson, there is the inn, between the grocer's shop and the bakery."

"I hope they have room for us," I replied.

"Have no fears on that score, old fellow. I took the precaution of wiring ahead to reserve our accommodation."

We were shown to two fine rooms overlooking the street. At luncheon, which comprised of chicken pie followed by a rather over-sweet gooseberry fool, Holmes mentioned his observation that the manager and staff seemed rather crestfallen.

"There is to be a funeral today, sir," our waiter said in answer to my friend's enquiry. "The deceased was a man known to all of us here in the village."

"I am exceedingly sorry to hear of this. May we know the poor fellow's name?"

"Of course, but it is unlikely that you will have encountered him, seeing as you are London gentlemen. He was Mr Ahab Rampling."

The shock from this news of the death of our client quickly passed, as I remembered his unhealthy appearance. Holmes' expression was unaltered, as he replied:

"I have indeed met Mr Rampling, in fact it is because of a business arrangement with him that we are here today. I recall that

23

he mentioned a number of unexpected deaths hereabouts when I spoke to him last, and expressed some concern regarding them. Do you, by any chance, recall the names of these unfortunates?"

The man gave us a slow, suspicious look. He brushed a stray lock of grey hair from his forehead.

"Mr Rampling was the manager of Sir Trevill Bertram's farm, sir. Sir Trevill owns most of the property around here, and I don't know that he would like me spreading our village affairs to outsiders."

Holmes raised his eyebrows. "I had no idea that he was so secretive. Ah well, no matter. I shall be seeing Sir Trevill later, so I expect he will tell me then."

"I didn't realise that you were acquainted with him, sir." The waiter's face reddened slightly, I noticed. "As far as I can recollect, three men and two women have passed away within the last month or so, including Mr Rampling. There was Thomas Leary, Matthew Collet, and Ben Trafford's wife as well as Arthur Edmond's sister. We thought at first that a plague had come upon us, but now it seems as if something in our food is the cause."

"Were that so, would not the deaths be more widespread?"

"Who knows, sir? Doctor Walgrave seems unable to discover the cause. Many of us are worried that we or our families will be the next to be struck down."

"Let us hope that both the cause and cure will be identified soon," I said. The waiter murmured his agreement and collected our coffee cups before leaving us.

"I think a word with Doctor Walgrave would be in order," Holmes said as we left the inn.

After asking directions from a passer-by we made our way up the High Street, past a number of shops and the church, turning into a narrow lane which rose steadily with occasional houses scattered around open fields. We had not walked far when we came to a thatched cottage surrounded by an array of colourful flowers. Holmes opened the white-painted gate and we approached the front door. As he raised his stick it swung open, to reveal a stern-looking woman, probably a secretary or receptionist I thought, who peered at us silently.

"Good afternoon," Holmes began, for it was past mid-day by now. "We would like to see Doctor Walgrave, if it is at all possible."

"I have not seen either of you before," she said haughtily.

"That is because we have not been here before. We are visitors."

"So you are not Doctor Walgrave's patients?"

"We are not."

"Are you in pain?"

"We are not," Holmes said again, in his most patient voice.

"Then what is your business here?"

"That is for the doctor and ourselves to discuss. My name is Sherlock Holmes, and I am in your charming village in response to a summons from the late Mister Ahab Rampling."

She looked from Holmes to me and back, clearly undecided as to whether to disturb the doctor.

"I, also, am a doctor," I added. "Kindly inform your employer that our purpose is of the utmost urgency."

"Very well." She vanished into the dim interior, leaving the door ajar.

Holmes glanced at me with raised eyebrows. He smiled faintly but said nothing.

"The doctor will see you. Come in," the woman said as she reappeared.

We allowed ourselves to be led along a short corridor and into a small room, lined with ancient books and containing a worn desk and chairs. The receptionist announced us and quickly retreated. Behind the desk stood an elderly man of distinguished appearance with hair and beard of pure white. His eyes were clear, as was his voice.

"I have heard of you and your companion, Mr Holmes. As you are a consulting detective, I assume you are here at the late Mr Rampling's bidding to attempt to discover the cause of our recent unexplained deaths, for he mentioned to me that he proposed to take some action. That is the case, is it not?"

"It is indeed, sir. I am told that it was first assumed that a plague had come upon the village."

"That was quickly disproved. At least as far as any plague that I am aware of is concerned." He gestured towards the chairs. "Let us sit, gentlemen."

We settled ourselves, the aged leather creaking under us. Doctor Walgrave sat hunched in his chair shaking his head hopelessly. After a moment, he looked up.

"I truly hope that you will be more successful than I. When I discounted plague from the possibilities, I turned to poison. I still believe that to be the cause, but I cannot identify it. My tests for arsenic and all other common substances of the kind have provided no answer, save that of elimination. This evening I shall take the train to Guildford, where I hope to consult a colleague who has spent some years in India. He has encountered many practices and cures that are strange to us, and may well be our last hope."

"If I may ask," I said, "what are the usual symptoms?"

"The patient appears extremely pale, as if drained of blood. A constant trembling, both of the body and voice, which rises and falls in its intensity. Speech becomes slow and uncertain and movement is maintained with increasing effort. The condition worsens within a few days, culminating in the ceasing of respiratory and kidney functions. Do you know of any poison that produces such effects, Doctor Watson?"

After brief consideration, I replied: "None that produce all of those symptoms. In Afghanistan, I recall, several preparations that produced similar effects were common among the natives but the paleness, especially, eludes me as to its source."

"Then we are no further advanced."

"Not as yet," Holmes acknowledged. "But tell me, do you know of any new cases in the village?"

"None have been reported to me since that of Mr Rampling."

My friend nodded. "Thank you, Doctor Walgrave, for allowing us to take up some of your valuable time." He rose abruptly. "I wish you well in Guildford, and with your further investigations."

"As I wish you, in yours," the doctor said.

#

We descended the hill with Holmes in deep thought. He walked with his head upon his chest and I said nothing until we were about to emerge into the High Street.

"Do you think that our friend the doctor will discover anything of worth in Guildford, Holmes?"

He gave a slight shrug. "I cannot answer such a question, because we do not know the nature of the poison or where its antidote is to be found. There is another way to solve this affair however, and that is to identify the poisoner and extract the information from him."

I was about to reply when Holmes touched my arm silently and pointed. A hearse had appeared, pulled by two black mares that seemed, from their slowness of movement, as downcast as the small procession of mourners who followed. We stood still, removing our hats and bowing our heads respectfully until the procession has passed. It had but a short distance to carry the coffin, which was visible within the brass rails of the bier, until it came to the churchyard further along the street.

Holmes looked especially grim.

"Cheer up, old fellow," I said by way of encouragement. "Though Mr Rampling has passed on, I have every hope that you will solve the problem he brought to you."

"I wonder, Watson, would he still be alive if I had begun to work on this case at once?"

I shook my head. "On that you can set your mind at rest, Holmes. Nothing that you, or I for that matter, could have done would have saved him. He had the appearance of a man at death's door. I fear that the poison is quite potent, even if its full effects are not felt immediately."

We continued our walk along the High Street in silence. Some of the shops were closed, doubtlessly because of the funeral, but the blacksmith was busy at his anvil. From behind us we heard running footsteps, and a moment later a large and surly-looking fellow who I recognised from the funeral procession caught up with us.

"Are you the detective from London?" he asked breathlessly.

"I am," my friend answered. "My name is Sherlock Holmes."

"Well, I am here to save you some trouble. I know that you are trying to find the cause of the deaths we've had hereabouts lately, but I can tell you here and now who is responsible."

"In that event, you will have solved the case for me. Pray tell me the identity of this murderer, for that he truly is."

The heaving of the man's massive chest began to subside. "It is my employer, Sir Trevill Bertram! He has been seen at night on his way to visit a witch, and has paid her to curse our village."

"But, even if that were possible, why would he do such a thing? Does Sir Trevill not own most of the village? It makes little sense to suppose that a man would deliberately bring about the end of some of his own tenants, surely."

"That may be so, but I know it. We all know it."

"Who are you, sir?"

"I am Roland Dender, the new farm manager. Sir Trevill appointed me on the day that Mr Rampling died."

"He is evidently not slow in managing his affairs, and this seems a curious way to show gratitude."

Mr Dender's eyes narrowed. "I told him months ago that it is I who should take care of things on the farm. Mr Rampling was slow with everything."

"You were not a friend of Mr Rampling's, then?"

"We had our disagreements."

"That is largely inevitable, when men work closely together for some time."

"Well, we fought once." Mr Dender was becoming uncomfortable I saw, now that he realised that he had not convinced Holmes. "I must go now. I have work to do."

With that he resumed his run, and was soon lost to our sight.

"It occurs to me, Holmes," I said as we resumed our walk, "that it could be that fellow who is at the root of this. He strikes me as rather insensitive, and he is clearly ruthlessly ambitious. He assumes Mr Rampling's position at the drop of a hat, so who is to say that he would flinch from taking over the entire farm? As he seems determined to throw suspicion upon Sir Trevill, to whom he should be grateful, it may be that there is some way, perhaps a clause in the landowner's will, that will enable him to achieve this."

"Certainly, that theory is worth considering," Holmes allowed, "and it may be that we will be forced to do so before this affair reaches its conclusion. However, I am inclined to believe that there is more to this." He stopped to examine a sign-post. "I see that the farm of Sir Trevill Bertram, whose name repeatedly confronts us, is only a mile or so further along this road. We will have a rather pleasant walk to there, I think, in the morning."

With that we returned to the inn. We sat in a quiet corner, where Holmes lit his pipe and maintained a thoughtful silence. I contented myself with a local newspaper until the hour for dinner arrived. My friend ate with more enthusiasm than usual, attacking his lamb and sprinkling it liberally with mint sauce. Our stewed apple dessert attracted less of his interest, but on completing our meal he called for two pints of good ale.

We returned to our former seats in the corner, and I noticed at once that he avoided any mention of or reference to our current investigation. This was a certain sign that Holmes had formed a theory, or perhaps more than one, and was testing them in his agile mind against the known facts. After a while he smiled and we reverted to discussing some of our old adventures, and to wondering what had befallen a few of our former clients. During our conversation our glasses had become empty and I made to signal the landlord, but my companion declined, saying that it was best that we retired a little early to be at our most alert in the morning.

I slept dreamlessly and woke to the loud crowing of a cock. By the time I had prepared myself and dressed I had heard movement outside my door, so I was not surprised to find that Holmes and one or two other guests were already taking breakfast as I entered the dining-room.

He greeted me cheerfully. "Good morning, Watson. I can recommend the kippers, if you are so disposed. Two of these and some toast should satisfy even your appetite until the time arrives for luncheon. As for me, I need nothing more except another pot of this strong coffee. Sit down, dear fellow, and I will summon the waiter."

This he did, and I ate heartily. On finishing our coffee he rose at once. "I think we will enjoy a pleasant walk to Sir Trevill Bertram's farm, as it is a bright and sunny morning. By now word of our presence will certainly have reached his ears, and I am curious as to the sort of reception we will receive."

As my friend had observed the previous day, it was little more than a mile from where the High Street became a tree-lined country lane to the entrance to the farm. We were then confronted with an uneven path that boasted the impression of many cart-wheels, with fields to either side in which villagers busily picked crops. Pigs, cows and sheep looked up from feeding to peer at us as we passed, and other, more distant, fields contained goats and several fine horses. The path continued past a group of outbuildings, one of them appearing to be a dairy, until it brought us to bushes fashioned to the shapes of animals spaced around a circular lawn. Beyond that a Tudor mansion stood, almost engulfed in ivy to the extent that the windows appeared as eyes staring from behind a mask.

"This is a strange place, Watson," Holmes remarked. "Observe the flags of many countries draped across most of the windows. I doubt if many men have travelled to such an extent. Also the suits of armour are, I would have thought, of too much value to a cultured man to be left outside to rust."

I glanced about me, around the courtyard and the front of the house. "Mr Rampling, I recall, mentioned his employer's bohemian ways, but this is not so much a home, as a museum."

The door opened before we reached the top of the steps to reveal a smiling butler, a tall man most of whose hair had been sadly lost, who welcomed us.

"Good morning, gentlemen. You are here to see Sir Trevill, of course. He is not at home now, but is expected back soon. Allow me to show you to the drawing-room, where I will serve port while you wait."

At his invitation we preceded him. He guided us to a room in which curtains hung half-drawn across tall windows and the furniture appeared fashioned from thick upholstered cane.

"Sir Trevill is evidently an explorer," Holmes remarked.

"Ah, Mr Holmes, you have noticed that the chairs are from foreign parts, and some of the trophies suggest this, perhaps. He has travelled much over the years, unlike myself who has yet to leave these shores." The butler bowed courteously. "My name is Morgan, gentlemen. If I can serve you in any way in my master's house, you have only to mention it."

"You know me, then?"

"Who has not heard of your most commendable fight against lawlessness?" He looked at me with kindly approval. "And of your excellent portrayal of these adventures, Doctor Watson. I confess to reading them as soon as they are published."

"I am glad that you find them entertaining," I replied.

"Oh, much more than that," he paused as he heard the clatter of horse's hooves from the courtyard. "But Sir Trevill has returned! He will be with you in a moment, I am sure, and I will serve drinks immediately."

"A rather familiar butler, wouldn't you say, Holmes?" I said when the man had left the room.

"He seems most content in his work, and lacks the aloofness that we are accustomed to."

"Quite. He is certainly well informed as to our activities."

"Doubtlessly your over-dramatic accounts of them have ensured this."

I scowled my disapproval of this most out-of-place and unnecessary remark, as our host arrived. He did not immediately greet us, but stood still and silent in momentary appraisal. At the same time I made my own assessment of the man, concluding that he was of a most bohemian nature as we had been told. His riding clothes were of a colourful tweed, such as you would not expect to be used for that purpose, and his greying hair touched his shoulders. His moustache was of an unusual style, his beard unkempt and his thick eyebrows gave him an almost menacing appearance. Quite suddenly, he smiled and approached us.

"Mr Sherlock Holmes and Doctor Watson! Morgan informed me, a moment ago, that you were here. I have just returned from a ride around the farm. Please sit, and tell me how I can assist you."

As we sank into two rather uncomfortable chairs, the butler entered with a tray. He filled three crystal glasses from a heavy decanter, handed them to us and departed. We sipped, and I tasted port of the finest quality.

"We have been summoned here by your late employee, Mr Ahab Rampling," Holmes began. "He reported several suspicious deaths in the village, and was convinced that they were not accidental. If you, yourself, have any opinions on this, or any additional information, it would be of immense help in our investigation."

Sir Trevill stroked his beard. "Rampling was an imaginative fellow, I often thought, but there has indeed been a surfeit of deaths hereabouts. As far as I am aware, neither Doctor Walgrave or Constable Jessop have found anything amiss, but the village is alive with rumours. Sometimes, one has difficulty in separating the truth from hearsay."

"So I understand, sir. We have heard mention of witchcraft and curses, hereabouts."

"Oh, that," our host dismissed the notion with a wave of his hand, and replaced his glass on the tray. "Those stories have been circulating here since the area first became a settlement, I shouldn't wonder. In particular, Barnabas Leary, the brother of one of the victims, is quite convinced of their veracity. In your place, gentlemen, I would discount such a consideration from my enquiries. The cause of the deaths of these poor unfortunates will probably become known in time, and will prove to be of a nature that is quite unexceptional."

Holmes and I put down our glasses and rose as one.

"My thanks to you for your time and hospitality," my friend said.

Sir Trevill smiled. "I fear I cannot have been of much help, but this interview I found most interesting. Pray feel free to visit my house again, should you acquire any insight on the situation that you feel you can share. Good morning, gentlemen."

Morgan appeared at the drawing-room door as if summoned by magic, and showed us out. Outside, as we were about to descend the steps, he confided to us:

"You gentlemen have doubtlessly heard of the stories surrounding Sir Trevill, commonly discussed in the village. It seems to me that there are some ungrateful souls in the area, when consideration is given to the employment he has provided, as well as the produce from the farm that he has distributed freely."

I was rather shocked by the man's references to his employer, although they were in no way derogatory. Holmes, however, maintained a thoughtful expression, saying only:

"Rumours are an unreliable basis on which to build opinions or theories, I have found. I perceive that you are content with your duties here, and that Sir Trevill appears satisfied with you. A mutually satisfactory situation, evidently."

The butler smiled and bowed as we turned away, and we soon found ourselves retracing our steps to Drewhampton.

"Sir Trevill seems like an amiable fellow after all, Holmes," I said when we had left the farm behind.

"So it would doubtless have appeared, had he not lied."

I slowed my pace and turned to him, aghast. "Whatever can you mean? I saw no deceit in the man."

"As always, Watson, you saw as I did, but you did not observe. You will recall his mention of riding around his estate."

"The farm, I believe he said."

"Quite so. You will doubtless recall that the entire area, the farmland and the land surrounding the house, was composed of a reddish soil, possibly because of a heavy clay content."

I nodded. "Indeed."

"Then it is difficult to see how one of Sir Trevill's boots could have had a fresh piece of black mud adhering to its sole, unless he had extended his ride a little further. When I add to this the rather defensive look he adopted as he explained his absence from the house, what am I to conclude, other than that he wishes to keep his wandering secret?"

"An assignation, perhaps? Possibly with one of the village girls?"

"That is certainly a possibility, but I dispensed with it because, to begin with, Sir Trevill must be in his late fifties. Also, he is aware of the dim view that some villagers have of him because of his supposed connection with witchcraft, even though no one can suggest a reason why he would wish harm to them. Why then, would he risk additional scandal that could cause some or all of his employees to seek positions elsewhere? Superstition is a powerful motivation, and I would wager that there are more than a few in the village that would prefer a longer journey to their work rather than the employment of a man they perceive as a wizard, let alone if he were also suspected of over-familiarity with their daughters. If sufficient resentment were caused, the farm could well face ruin."

"What then, do you believe that he is concealing?"

We had by this time almost reached the inn. A cart, piled high with hay, made its way past slowly.

"That, we may discover tonight," Holmes replied as we crossed the road opposite the entrance. "But, as it is time for luncheon, let us now eat and refresh ourselves. This afternoon we will seek additional information about Sir Trevill's conduct from another source."

#

During our meal I noticed that my friend's eyes were now filled with a look that I was long familiar with. He had, I knew, begun to piece together the disparate elements of this case, recognising clues that were quite beyond me. After our long association I should have become accustomed to his ways, but there were still many times when I felt in awe of his intellect.

"What is it that you intend for this afternoon?" I enquired as we finished our meal.

He glanced around the dining-room to confirm that we could not be overheard. "You will recall, Watson, that Sir Trevill mentioned the brother of one of his tenants, Barnabas Leary. I am inclined to seek this man's viewpoint on the deaths in the village, and on the reason for his suspicions."

We rose then and made to leave, but Holmes waited until the waiter appeared. He asked the fellow a question, to which the answer was quickly forthcoming.

"So, Watson, we now know that Mr Leary resides at 9, Wheatsheaf Copse," he explained. "In a small village such as this it is certain that a person's business, and indeed where he may be found, is known to almost everyone. As with most destinations hereabouts, ours is within walking distance."

A fifteen minute walk, in the opposite direction to that we had set out upon that morning, brought us to a lane that was awash with wild flowers. I wondered, for a moment, if this was the place we sought, but my friend confirmed this by peering beneath the heavily-leafed branches that obscured a sign-post.

"But there are no houses to be seen, Holmes. There are nothing but fields and animals within our sight."

He viewed our surroundings. "Then we have no alternative than to follow this most scenic thoroughfare until we come upon some signs of habitation. Do not despair, old fellow, I have every expectation that around this bend will be the house that we seek."

In no more than a minute, he was proven correct. After a short but brisk walk that took us around a long curve, the trees and flowers gave way to a cluster of about a dozen small dwellings. At our approach Holmes inspected the cottages and, finding no numbers, he counted from the first before rapping on a rather dilapidated door.

Presently it opened a few inches, and an eye peered out from the gloom within.

"Mr Barnabas Leary?" enquired Holmes. "My name is Sherlock Holmes and this is my associate, Doctor John Watson.

We would be grateful if you would spare us a few minutes of your time, sir."

"What is this about?" The door opened further.

"As well as expressing our condolences regarding your brother, we would like to ask you about the owner of the farm hereabouts, Sir Trevill Bertram. He has featured greatly in our investigation into the sudden deaths that have occurred in the village of late, and we are given to believe that you hold that he is some way responsible. "

Now the door opened wider, revealing a short elderly man with wild hair and a sullen expression.

"That man is a servant of the devil!" He exclaimed. "Who else can be the cause of Thomas' death and of Ben Trafford's wife's passing, or that of Arthur Edmond's sister, not to mention Mr Rampling and Matthew Collet? I tell you, three men and two women, all good and sturdy folk, have been taken from us."

By now it was apparent that we were not to be invited into Mr Leary's home but this, if it occurred to him at all, did not deter Holmes in his questioning.

"Pray enlighten us as to your reason for this accusation."

"Thomas worked on the land for more than twenty years," the old man growled, "and he always swore that Sir Trevill went out every evening to consort with a witch or to visit some sort of cult that worships the devil. He never told me how that became known or who confided it to him, but it's been common knowledge around here for a long time and that usually means it's the truth. I can tell you that there's any number of folk who would leave his employ if they could but there's no other estate within miles, and work on the land is all they know." His tone calmed slightly. "In fairness though, I don't think the wages would be as good, anyway."

Holmes nodded thoughtfully. "And you cannot tell us how such a suspicion began?"

"There was a story that was heard in the village for a little while, some years ago," Mr Leary remembered. "It was told by an animal doctor who was called to the farm to treat some sick cows. The way he put it, as he arrived one evening he walked from the station and, not being familiar with the village, went out of his way. Soon he saw a man enter the house of an old and evil-looking woman over on the Guilford Road. From what he said, it appeared as if they knew each other and acted quite familiar. The doctor stayed at the inn that night, where he related his experience to other customers who he had struck up a friendship with. The next morning he arrived at the farm and found, to his surprise, that the man he had seen the previous evening was none other than Sir Trevill!

"Now, Mr Holmes, when he was working late it didn't take Thomas long to realise that his employer strode off in that direction every evening at about the same time, which was about eight o'clock. I know that us village folk are said to be simple and superstitious, but if you add to what I've just said to the well-known fact that Sir Trevill never is anything but prosperous, regardless of the richness of the harvest or anything else, and then you remember the saying that the devil looks after his own, it's easy to see, isn't it, how his reputation came to be?"

"Indeed, there is no mystery about it," Holmes said wryly. "I thank you, Mr Leary. Your information has been most helpful. I would not be surprised if Sir Trevill's activities were not clear to all, in the very near future. Good day to you, sir."

We retraced our steps with Holmes saying little. He walked with his head upon his chest, as he always did when pondering the facts and inferences of a current case. When he began to give his attention to his surroundings, at first to the colourful variety of plants and flowers and then to the passers-by in the street, I ventured to interrupt his thoughts.

"I take it, Holmes, that you have dismissed Mr Leary's viewpoint on this matter. It seems to me that he believes the superstition that has been attached to Sir Trevill, which appears to be little more than local gossip. I do not feel that we have learned much, here."

Holmes nodded slowly. "Gossip, yes, although I do not always dismiss this a source of information. I think Watson, that we will return to the inn to spend an hour or two smoking peacefully, before dinner. Then we will set about ascertaining the true reason for Sir Trevill's nightly excursions. I feel we must clarify his intentions before proceeding further, although I do not expect them to be in any way the cause of the villagers' deaths."

"You are quite certain that he is in no way connected with these occurrences, then?"

"I have been, almost from the first. Despite all opinions to the contrary I can see no reason for such actions, despite the mud on his boots that I noticed previously. However, our exercise tonight will either confirm or deny my suppositions"

I can recall making but one remark to Holmes, during a quite acceptable dinner which he regarded with little interest.

"There appear to be no hansoms around the village, but perhaps we can hire a cart for the evening."

He laced his long fingers together, after pushing his half-empty plate away.

"Why ever should we do that, old fellow?"

"To follow Sir Trevill, of course."

"That will not be necessary, I think." He folded his napkin and placed it before him. "You will recall that Mr Barnabas Leary related that his brother often watched his employer as he strode off, on his nightly travels. From this we can expect that the journey is a short one. I'll wager that the Guildford Road is quite near at hand."

So it proved to be. We had hardly finished our coffee, before Holmes stood up with an expression of anticipation upon his face.

We set up a brisk pace as the light faded quickly, and by the time we had reached the farm darkness was complete. The place presented no difficulty as to our entry, for the wide gate was secured only by a latch that was within easy reach. We kept to the shadows, watching for any workers who might still be nearby, and hearing only the murmur of animal sounds and the sighing of the slight wind among the trees. When the house was in sight, my friend silently guided me away from the path.

"If Sir Trevill wishes to keep his excursions secret, he will doubtlessly leave by a back door," he whispered.

Accordingly, we settled ourselves in the concealment of a thick bush that grew near both a rear entrance and the path that led further into the estate. Fortunately, the night was warm enough for us to be comfortable, and very soon we heard the faint chimes of the church clock in the village. I took out my pocket-watch and saw that the next fifteen minutes would bring us to eight o'clock.

Sir Trevill was indeed a punctual man, for he appeared exactly as the clock struck the hour. We crouched still as statues, holding our breath as his indistinct form marched past with the gravel crunching beneath his boots.

"Not yet, Watson. Wait." My friend placed a restraining hand on my shoulder as I made to rise. When all sounds had ceased we rose slowly and I followed Holmes to the rear of the estate in close pursuit. The shadowy figure of Sir Trevill strode unhesitatingly ahead, and not once did he look back. Under the trees the darkness was dense, but Holmes seemed to see ahead with much more clarity than I. It was in far less time than I expected that we came upon a low fence, and after crossing a rather dilapidated stile found ourselves in a field edged by a narrow footpath.

We halted abruptly as Sir Trevill paused, for fear of becoming close. The cry of an owl, no doubt surprised at our sudden appearance, and the rustle of leaves intruded briefly into the silence. Then he continued until another stile confronted him, before crossing into the deserted Guildford Road.

Holmes held up a hand in a silent gesture, and we halted to watch Sir Trevill walk a final few yards to where a small cluster of cottages stood in darkness. We hesitated while he approached, and it was only as the door of the nearest of them was answered to his knock that we emerged.

"Good evening, Sir Trevill," my friend called as we drew nearer.

The landowner turned towards us quickly. "Good heavens! Mr Holmes and Doctor Watson." Then his expression clouded, as he was struck by realisation. "Did you follow me here, sirs?" He asked angrily.

Before either Holmes or myself could reply, the figure standing in the shadow of the doorway spoke softly to Sir Trevill. He answered soothingly, before returning his attention to us.

"I imagine that you gentlemen seek confirmation of the absurd rumours that circulate among my tenants. I know of the things that the villagers say about me but I have yet to discover their reason, if it is other than primitive superstition. Very well then, you shall have your explanation." He paused and in that instant the shape before him moved, so that the meagre light from the candle within revealed a very elderly lady whose skin appeared yellowed and wrinkled like ancient parchment. Despite her obviously painful condition, she smiled at us as she was introduced as Miss Gwendolyn Stirk.

We replied courteously, and Sir Trevill continued.

"This lady is no witch, gentlemen. She is, in fact, my aunt. Her unfortunate condition is the result of nursing the poor in India, where she was for many years attached to a religious order. She has been a good and charitable women for all of her life, but now is in need of my help in order to survive. She chooses to live a lonely existence because she fears that the disease she carries might be passed to others, although I have attempted many times to persuade her otherwise since I am unaffected. Far from taking offence at the locals' accusation, she finds them amusing. I, however, do not."

An expression that I have rarely seen crossed Holmes' face, to quickly disappear.

"Sir Trevill," he said then, "I cannot but apologise for this intrusion, to both Miss Stirk and yourself." He paused as I mumbled my concurrence. "But you will, I am certain, appreciate that my work demands that every avenue in question should be explored. By way of restitution I will, if you both agree, arrange for Sir James Saunders, the London dermatologist, to visit you, Miss Stirk, to make a thorough examination. I have some slight acquaintance with Sir James, and it is certain that this would take place before too long, and that he would quickly ascertain whether or not your fears are justified. I beg that you consider this."

Sir Trevill looked to his aunt who, after some hesitation, nodded silently.

"Very well," he said again. "We will discuss your proposition. If you would be so good as to call on me in the morning, I will tell you of our decision." His long hair glinted in the poor light. "Goodnight to you gentlemen."

#

We retraced out steps rather more slowly. I felt relieved to be back among the trees and surrounded by silence.

"I am afraid we have committed a cardinal error there, Holmes," I said presently.

"Much to the contrary, old fellow. Everything has worked out exactly as I expected."

I turned to him in surprise, hardly able to distinguish his shape in the gloom. "I cannot see how that can be."

"It is really quite simple. As you know, I give no credence to the supernatural, so the elderly woman featured in the various reports concerning Sir Trevill's night time visits seemed to me most likely to be either infirm or in some way ill. I could not of course define the exact circumstances, but I was reasonably certain that I would be able to offer assistance in the shape of one or other of the London specialists that have become known to me over the years. Had they declined my help I would have found some way to insist, and if they had made an immediate decision I would have suggested they sleep on it, for it was imperative that Sir Trevill invite us to call at his home tomorrow."

I stopped, a little breathless, and placed my hand against a sturdy oak for support. "But what can we hope to discover? Is there more to Sir Trevill's part in this, after all?"

"No, Watson." Holmes stood a few feet away and lit his pipe, but you will recall the butler, Morgan."

"Rather a forward fellow, I thought."

"That is as may be, but did you notice the tattoo on his right wrist?"

I thought for a moment. "I seem to remember the mathematical symbol, known as "pi", and concluding that he may have at some time been a teacher of that subject."

"Not so, old fellow, but almost correct. In fact you have mistaken the Greek letter for a Mandarin character. In spite of his assertion that he has never left this land, this shows clearly that Morgan has at some time visited China."

"But that design could have been applied to him anywhere. There are establishments in Limehouse that specialise in such things."

"Indeed there are, but his tattoo came from the Orient."

I smiled, but yet I knew that he would never joke about his observations.

"Holmes, how could you know that?"

"You will disappoint me, Watson, if you tell me that you have forgotten a previous client, Mr Jabez Wilson. If you remember, from my previous study of tattoos I was able to identify his as Chinese by its distinctive colouring. The same is true of that of Morgan. Examples from elsewhere have a lighter colour."

"Yet he mentioned, for no apparent reason, that he has never been there, or to any other country for that matter. Yes, I see."

"That is why, old friend, for the purpose of confirmation we will visit the tiny library that I observed next to that rather luridly-painted tea shop just off Drewhampton High Street. If we set off immediately after breakfast, we should still be able to reach Sir Trevill's house quite early."

In the library the following morning Holmes selected and began to pore over a volume about ancient Chinese medicine, while I contented myself with a back issue of a medical journal. Less than half an hour had passed before he stood up, closing the book and returning it to its place. Quietly, we thanked the librarian for his help in directing us to our chosen subjects, and immediately set off for our appointment with Sir Trevill.

"Did you find what you expected, Holmes?" I enquired.

"Exactly that. Everything is now clear to me. It remains only to send a wire from the Post Office, and my case is complete."

We said little until we reached our destination. I knew better than to ask my friend about his discoveries in the library, or about his deductions. He would reveal all at the appropriate time, and that could not be far away.

Morgan positively radiated good humour as he admitted us.

"Welcome again, gentlemen. Sir Trevill forewarned me of your visit, and instructed me to see that you are comfortable until he returns from his ride. He will not be long. I would say no more than half an hour."

We thanked him and allowed ourselves to be led into the drawing room as before.

"The truth is, Morgan, that on this occasion we are here to see you, as much as Sir Trevill," Holmes said as we seated ourselves.

The butler's expression went blank, suddenly. "Me, sir? How could that possibly be?"

"That I will explain presently. For now I will prevail upon you to bring to us the telegram that will arrive at any moment."

Morgan bowed. "Of course, sir. Meanwhile I will bring porter and some of the seed cake that our village is famous for. I trust that will be acceptable?"

"Most certainly," I answered, as Holmes nodded.

As soon as we were alone Holmes inclined his head to listen, I perceived, for the retreating footsteps of the butler.

"At all costs, Watson," he whispered, "touch nothing. Do not eat as much as a crumb, nor drink a drop."

I was about to reply when Morgan reappeared. He placed a laden tray before us, containing generous quantities of cake and port.

"I am most curious," he said to Holmes, "as to what it is that you wish to speak of to me. I believe – but there is the door-bell ringing. Doubtlessly it is the telegraph boy."

He left us again, and returned in moments. Holmes tore open the envelope held out to him on a tray.

"Now I will tell you," he looked straight at Morgan with triumph in his face. "that I have concluded my investigation. There is but one unanswered question, which only you can settle."

Some of the geniality had left the butler's face. "Whatever could that be?"

"The reason why you have poisoned three men and two women in the village of Drewhampton."

If we expected this to be received with some excitement, we were disappointed.

"I did not think of any of this as humorous, sir," Morgan said calmly. "Allow me to cut you a piece of this seed cake, to sustain you until Sir Trevill's return."

"I imagine you knew," Holmes continued, "from your travels in China, that the gu poison is obtained from venomous snakes which are imprisoned with lethal scorpions in a jar. The survivor of the resulting fights is used to obtain the substance which you have employed. No doubt you were a member of a cult that disposes of its victims in this way, either for revenge or money. I confess that I had no indication of this, until I eventually realised the significance of your tattoo."

Morgan glanced at his wrist. "Surely you are mistaken."

"The discovery that the same device has been the symbol of the cult from ancient times makes this unlikely, I think."

"Gentlemen," the tray was held within easy reach of both of us, "do try this cake. I find it quite delicious."

To my amazement Morgan then took a slice and consumed it before us, a highly unusual liberty for a servant but, I suspected, intended to demonstrate that the cake was free of poison. It flashed across my mind that it could have been the act of a guilty man cheating the hangman, but he seemed unaffected.

"I will, I think, forego that pleasure," Holmes answered.

At that moment several things occurred. Morgan's expression changed as he accepted defeat. The mask slipped. The good humour vanished in an instant, to be replaced by the grim countenance and soulless eyes of a man who feels no remorse. Behind him I saw the drawing-room door open to admit Sir

Trevill, who was accompanied by another. I started as I recognised Inspector Lestrade.

Morgan became very still as he realised that we were no longer alone. He turned his head slowly, and then his body seemed to sag before us.

"Good morning, Sir Trevill!" Holmes cried jovially. "I do hope you intend to accept my offer of last night. Ah, I see that Lestrade accompanies you! You have arrived remarkably quickly, Inspector. I commend you."

Sir Trevill nodded but said nothing, as Morgan squirmed visibly under his condemning stare.

"I came as soon as I could, Mr Holmes," Lestrade said. "Just managed to catch the morning train. I consulted the archives at the Yard, and had one of my men wire the Chief Constable of Surrey as you suggested."

"I was right, then?" My friend enquired.

"Oh, you were, sir. It's been five years now, but I soon uncovered the truth."

"As I knew you would, Inspector. I take it that you happened to meet Sir Trevill on your way from the station, and recognised him from my description."

"That I did. I explained to him some of what has been going on hereabouts, and he brought me here at once."

"Capital! Perhaps you would care to elaborate on your findings, for the further understanding of Sir Trevill and Doctor Watson."

Lestrade acknowledged me courteously, before he spoke. "The Northern Landworkers Bank robbery, of five years or so ago, was a dreadful affair. An official was shot dead, as were two police officers who attempted to arrest the robbers. The gang, five of them, fled south from Northumberland with the intention of taking a boat to escape to France. When this proved impossible because of the nation-wide manhunt and days of bad weather, they hid in various towns, always on the move, until they finally settled in Drewhampton."

"Attracted by its quietness and because it is situated off the beaten track, so to speak," I remarked.

"Exactly, Doctor. Each of the robbers found lodgings in the village, intending to remain here until things settled down. I regret that I have been unsuccessful in discovering whether any of the villagers concerned knowingly harboured the fugitives in exchange for money. This state of affairs might have continued for much longer had not a certain Mrs Molly Wixted somehow discovered the truth about them. She was a married woman from Kent, who had taken refuge here from a violent husband. One of the gang is thought to have murdered her, for she was found strangled after their departure."

Holmes turned to Sir Trevill. "Was it not about this time when Morgan took up his position with you?" he asked.

"It was," the landowner looked at Morgan through narrowed eyes. "His predecessor, Boone, had disappeared, failing to return from a short visit to his relatives in Bristol. After several days Morgan presented himself, explaining that he was a cousin of Boone who had died suddenly from a weak heart. I have not doubted this, until now. Morgan claimed that he, like several members of Boone's family, was experienced in the profession, and so I accepted him on a trial basis at first, as a replacement. His references were impressive."

"Forged, doubtlessly," Lestrade said.

Holmes nodded. "Tell us then, Inspector, of the connection of Morgan to this affair."

"This Mrs Wixted was his sister, and revenge for her death was the sole reason for his presence in the village, and for taking up employment with Sir Trevill. My enquiries have revealed that the first villager was murdered on the fifth anniversary of her death."

"Thank you, Inspector," Holmes said. "So you, Morgan, allowed a year to elapse for each intended victim. That, I imagine, was in order that your activities would not be connected to the events of five years ago. I am aware that you have travelled in the Orient where you became familiar with gu, a local poison much used by criminals thereabouts but unknown otherwise. How, by the way, did you administer it?"

Morgan raised his head from his chest, sullen-faced. "Since you and the inspector seem to have become acquainted with my plan, Mr Holmes, it can do no harm to tell you. One of my duties as Sir Trevill's butler was to take messages and instructions to the farm and the adjoining dairy. It was a simple matter to ascertain which milk churns were to be delivered to the villagers who had harboured those robbers, and whose actions had led to my sister's death, and then to add a little powder before they were sealed."

"But two of your victims were women!" Sir Trevill exclaimed.

"They were incidental," Morgan said contemptuously. "How was I to know if it was the man or the woman of the house who had allowed those murderers to remain there? To me, their punishment was equally satisfying."

"You may yet cheat the hangman. It may be an asylum for you." Lestrade murmured.

Morgan smiled crookedly, an expression that made his madness evident. "But you will prove none of this, in court. I have enough money saved for the services of the best lawyers in the land. What is my confession? A fairy tale that I invented to amuse you. Nothing more."

"There is, I think, one piece of evidence that cannot be explained away easily," Holmes asserted.

"Impossible! My plan was perfect."

My friend went to the tray containing the seed cake. "It did not escape my notice that you were excessively anxious, as soon as you realised that I had identified you as the murderer of the villagers, to ensure that I consumed some of this cake." He withdrew the knife that had sliced the confection and handed it to Lestrade. "I will wager, Inspector, that it will be found that the blade is smeared with the very poison that we have been discussing."

"But Holmes, Morgan himself ate some of it." I pointed out.

"It is a very old trick, Watson, dating as far back as the Borgias unless I am much mistaken. Only the unfortunate who partakes from some of the food is affected. The blade, you see, is coated on one side only."

"Devilishly ingenious," Sir Trevill gasped.

Lestrade stepped forward and firmly handcuffed Morgan's wrists. "Come on, my lad. It's the local lock-up for you, until the next train to London arrives."

"That should be in precisely two hours and twenty minutes, Inspector," Holmes said after consulting his pocket-watch.

"Thank you, Mr Holmes and Doctor Watson, for your assistance."


"We are always glad to be of service. However, Watson, I perceive that you are about to mention that the time for luncheon approaches, and the inn is serving a particularly well-seasoned partridge. Perhaps, after your visit to the local station, you would care to join us, Inspector?"

The Adventure of The Returning Spirit

I will always remember a day in November 1894, as one of the worst in my life. More painful, in its way, even than my experiences in Maiwand.

As I trudged up the stairs of my former lodgings in Baker Street the cloud of gloom and depression surrounding me seemed, if anything, denser even than the night before. Sleep had eluded me, and thoughts of grief and uncertainty had proved haunting companions, so that I resolved to seek the advice and wisdom of my friend, Mr Sherlock Holmes, immediately after my poor attempt at consuming breakfast.

"Watson!" He greeted me with apparent delight as I entered our old sitting room.

"Good morning, Holmes. You sound, if I may say so, rather cheerful. You have, perhaps, gained a new client?"

"Not so, old fellow, my mood has been elevated by a prolonged Turkish bath. I returned here not half an hour ago and....' His eyes swept over me and he became very still. "But what is it? I perceive that you are not yourself today. Are you ill?"

I took off my hat and coat and sat down, not in my usual armchair but in the basket chair. "Holmes, I am besieged by melancholia. I apologise for visiting you in this state, but I feel a strong need for human company this morning."

He was beside me at once, lowering himself into the nearest armchair. "My dear fellow, it is usually I, not yourself, who is afflicted in this way. What is it that has brought it upon you again?

When I returned to London you were still suffering from the loss of your wife, but I formed the impression that you had managed to come to terms with it, and had almost recovered."

"You were not mistaken. The pain of grief had begun to fade, and your reappearance was a welcome distraction."

"Then what is it that troubles you now?" He leaned closer, his concerned expression deepening. "Pray tell me. If anything can be done to assist, you have only to mention it."

"Thank you, Holmes, but there is nothing that any man can do."

"It is still the loss of Mrs Watson that haunts you, then?"

"It is, but there is more."

Holmes got to his feet. "You must tell me all, but first a brandy to steady your nerves."

"It is too early, I think."

"Nonsense. You are in need of a restorative. Time has nothing to do with it."

He took up a crystal glass and poured from the decanter. I let the harsh spirit burn my throat and then calm me gradually. By the time I was ready to speak, I did indeed feel somewhat improved. As I prepared myself to begin, the only sounds were of passing hansoms and four-wheelers. Then raucous laughter floated up through the half-open window, and faded as two young men strode by and were quickly out of earshot.

"I saw her, or so it appeared, last night as I returned to Kensington. It was late, my patient's fever did not break until early evening."

"You saw Mrs Watson?"

"I did, Holmes, as clearly as I now see you."

"Old friend, you are a medical man and not usually given to fantasies," he said gently. "Do not torment yourself, for you know this cannot be so."

"She called to me."

"As I recall, there was a fog last evening, the thickest for weeks. Looking from this window, I was unable to see the street below. Such a setting, especially if you had allowed your mind to dwell upon your loss, could have fired your imagination."

I spent a few moments, breathing deeply in my frustration. "Holmes, I am aware of your total disbelief in the supernatural and I have usually held a similar view, but I swear to you that I saw and heard Mary last night as if she were still alive."

He sat back in his chair, now regarding me with a thoughtful expression. "Very well, Watson. Relate to me exactly the scene that you witnessed. I cannot believe that the departed, however much they are loved, can return, but I see trickery in this. As to the reason behind it I cannot yet tell, but we will see what results from a little reasoning."

"I was almost at my front door," I said when I had collected my thoughts, "as a coach appeared out of the fog. I heard the horses' hooves and then saw faintly the glow of the side-lamps. It slowed its pace, which I dismissed as a necessity because of the greatly restricted visibility, and it was then that I heard a woman's voice calling my name. She identified herself as Mary, saying that she had returned and would be with me again soon. No sooner had I taken this in, that the coach was lost to my sight."

"Was the voice that of your wife, as you remember it?"

"It could have been, allowing for some slight distortion caused by the fog."

"And the woman's appearance?"

"As far as I could tell, it was she."

"Because of the fog and the shock this would have been to you, I can understand that you would not have thought to take note of the coach's number although, of course, it could have been a private conveyance. But what of the coachman? Were you able to see his face clearly, perhaps recognise him?"

I shook my head. "I had an impression of a vague figure, possibly clad in a black rain-cape with the collar turned up to conceal his face. The apparition appeared and was gone, so quickly."

Holmes nodded slowly. "Is there anything more that you can tell me?"

"There is. This morning I received a note. It was in my letter-box and delivered by hand. It said simply, 'John, I will soon be with you again'."

"Do you have it with you?"

I nodded and withdrew the crumpled sheet from my pocket.

Holmes studied it for a moment, then produced his lens. "Poor quality paper, rather pale ink written with a well-used nib. The handwriting is indeed a woman's, but that is as far as I will go with your assertions." His voice took on a softer tone. "Watson, you must know that this is some sort of cruel trick. There are no such things as ghosts or returning spirits. How many times have we been confronted with cases that appeared to be concerned with the supernatural, only to finally discover a perfectly ordinary down-to-earth solution? Ask yourself, do ghosts leave notes in your letter-box? Consider this also, would this have affected you so, were you not still grieving for your departed wife? Ordinarily, you would have immediately identified the situation for what it is, would you not?"

I allowed his words to impress themselves upon my mind. After a moment, I had collected myself sufficiently to realise the sense of his statements, and the foolishness of my gullibility. There have been times however, when I have seen things that could not be explained. I mentioned this to Holmes.

"Old fellow," he began after a pause, "you must not underestimate the power or versatility of the human imagination. Additionally, the eyes do not always reveal accurately what is before us. Light and shade, mirrors and suggestion can all play their part in deceiving us. However, that deals with past experience. What we have here is, as I have said, nothing more than human trickery. Tell me, after such a shock, do you feel you can conduct your practice today?"

I straightened my posture, feeling rather like a man emerging from a confused dream.

"You are right of course, Holmes, about everything. I must take myself in hand. I have to collect myself and open my surgery." I reflected, briefly. "Sometimes it is the little things that you remember when you think of a lost loved one, that are the most painful by their absence. The way she arranged my slippers, my pipe and my book in readiness for me to sit with her before the fire on winter evenings, are memories that I will always keep."

"I am, as you are aware, unacquainted with such emotions," Holmes said, and I wondered if I imagined the touch of sadness in his voice, "but it grieves me to see your distress." He paused, and I formed the impression that something had occurred to him. "There is at this time a case of momentous importance before me, which I expect to break within a day or two. Nevertheless, Watson, if you depart now to attend your practice I will attempt to gain some insight into these extraordinary events. I suggest that you call here after closing your surgery this afternoon, when I hope to be able to enlighten you somewhat."

I murmured my thanks to my friend. Then, still in a troubled state, I set out to return to Kensington and what seemed to be an endless stream of patients.

#

The day proved to be as unremarkable as I had feared, with little to take my mind from the images that haunted me. Among the legions of influenza cases, children with measles and the elderly suffering a myriad of complaints, were some who remarked that I seemed preoccupied or enquired about my state of health. Relief descended upon me like a cloud, as I finally closed my surgery doors in the late afternoon.

I quickly found a hansom nearby, and was back in Baker Street soon after. Mrs Hudson gave me a concerned look as she admitted me, but it was the tone of her greeting that told me how obvious my distressed state must appear.

As I ascended the stairs the mournful wail of Holmes' Stradivarius matched my mood. I hoped that my friend had discovered something that would lift my depression.

"Ah, Watson, my dear fellow." He replaced his violin in its case and came to greet me. Somewhat excessively, I thought. He seemed in a light-hearted mood, probably for my sake. "Do sit down, while I call for our good landlady to bring tea."

I was about to tell him it was unnecessary, but thought better of it. Mrs Hudson must have been waiting for his summons, for she appeared more quickly even than is usual. She avoided my eyes, but there was pain in her face. She never failed to be concerned, when Holmes or I suffered injury or distress.

He said little while we drank, but scrutinized me constantly. "I suppose you can think of no one who would wish you harm," he said suddenly.

"I received a letter from Doctor Bolt, yesterday. He accuses me regularly of poaching his patients and issues veiled threats, but I never take that seriously. I am afraid that his increasing absent-mindedness is the reason for his declining practice. In any event, I cannot see a man of his age arranging something of this sort."

"Most unlikely, I am certain. If you had any lingering doubts about your experiences being anything but a despicable trick, you can dispel them completely," my friend said then. "The results of my enquiries suggest that you are not the only intended victim. I fear we are both to suffer, if the perpetrator is allowed to continue."

"What can you mean, Holmes? Have you discovered who is behind this?"

"Not as yet, but I suspect that our adversary is he who drove the coach that so alarmed you last night. However, I first concerned myself with the woman who impersonated Mrs Watson. It occurred to me that she is most likely accustomed to taking on the appearance of others, since she appeared so convincing. My starting point therefore, was to investigate within the theatrical profession. You may recall that I have consulted Miss Gloriana Roland before, at the Imperial Theatre where her play is enjoying an extended run. After examining the tiny portrait of your late wife which I borrowed from where you left it in your former room, she was able to supply me with the names and whereabouts of four actresses known to her who could have assumed her identity. I spent the remainder of the morning and some of the afternoon in eliminating three from the list, leaving me with Miss Agnes Bowman, of King Alfred Square, St John's Wood."

I have long been acquainted with Holmes' methods, but I was surprised at his rapid progress and doubly appreciative of his assistance. "Have you interviewed this woman?"

"It seemed more advantageous to delay the encounter. I thought you might care to accompany me this evening, to see for yourself that she is merely flesh and blood. Miss Roland has explained that Miss Bowman is at present between parts since her last production proved unsuccessful, so we have a good chance of finding her at home."

"Holmes, I am most grateful to you."

"Think nothing of it. Incidentally, I have informed Mrs Hudson that you will be staying for dinner. I hope I was not presumptuous?"

"Not at all," I replied, feeling suddenly in a lighter frame of mind. "At this moment, I can think of nothing I would like better."

#

We stood at the entrance to King Alfred Square, a small enclave in Grove End Road that was sparsely lit by the pale glow of several street-lamps. The villas were of uniform appearance, some of them brightly illuminated from within but most in darkness. After taking a moment or two to survey his surroundings, Holmes strode forward. By his side, I asked which house we were bound for.

"I believe Miss Roland gave the number as twenty-eight," he said, peering around us. "Ah, there is number thirty, so this is Miss Bowman's home two houses further on."

We approached a door with an ornate knocker in the shape of an elephant's head which Holmes ignored, rapping urgently on the thick panels with his cane. There was no response. He repeated the summons and we listened for any sound of activity within.

"Either she is not inside, or she wishes us to believe that," he whispered. "Perhaps the view from the back of the house will be more enlightening."

I preceded him to the wooden gate at the side of the villa, which opened easily as I lifted the latch. We passed silently into a paved passage that led to the back of the house. Holmes stared through a small window into the shadows of the kitchen. A row of saucepans hung from a rack immediately ahead, obstructing our view. He changed his angle of observation several times, until he could see through a half-open door into the room beyond. The light was minimal, but his sharp eyes must have seen something immediately, for he turned to me urgently.

"Someone is there. We must enter, Watson."

There was apparently no further need for stealth, for he produced his pick-lock and opened the door in seconds without attempting to maintain silence. He rushed through the kitchen and into the living-room and I followed close behind, but a single glance told me that the woman within was beyond my help.

"Whoever did this was particularly brutal," I observed.

Miss Agnes Bowman was sprawled across an armchair, in which she had been occupied with embroidery. Her mouth was open and her eyes bulged, adding to the terrible expression that was frozen upon her face. The cause of her death was apparent, for a thin wire had been wound around her neck and tightened to the extent that it had become embedded in the bloody flesh. Despite my long experience of death and injury, I felt myself shiver.

"How long, would you say?" Holmes asked.

I moved closer, and carefully felt the stiffened flesh. The blood had long since dried. "At least twelve hours."

"She had served her purpose and was of no further use. Doubtlessly she knew too much about her murderer, and he could not risk her divulging anything that could lead to his capture."

"You are certain that it was a man?"

"Not absolutely, but the strength required to sink the wire into this unfortunate woman's neck to this depth strongly suggests it."

"And you believe she was killed by someone of her acquaintance?"

"I will confirm that in a moment." He retraced his steps into the yard. After a short search of the single patch of coarse grass he gave a cry of satisfaction and returned holding up a key for my inspection. "He evidently entered with her consent, probably by the front door, since there is no damage anywhere. He left, locking the kitchen door and throwing away the key. That patch of grass is the only possible place of concealment at the rear of the house."

I picked up the oil lamp and turned up the wick before bringing it nearer to the body. "Holmes, this cannot be the woman who impersonated Mary. The colour of her hair is similar, but her features are quite different."

"Indeed it appears so, but notice the almost identical shape of the head and particularly the nose. I have some experience of such things, and I can tell you confidently that a skilful master of his craft would be capable of transforming her into an acceptable likeness, especially when viewed from a distance."

I exhaled deeply, feeling a strange relief despite the circumstances. "At least, there is now some explanation."

"For the simulated reappearance of your wife, yes. We must of course telegraph Lestrade after leaving here, but already I have my suspicions."

"You have formed a supposition?"

"I have, but for the moment it is no more than that. However, we will inform the good inspector and he will come to his own conclusions. I am now certain that I, as well yourself, am an intended victim in this affair."

I considered, but could not fathom his reasoning. "How so, Holmes?"

He began to scrutinize the room carefully. "I will tell you presently, if I am proven correct." He shook his head, appearing disappointed. "He was careful, it seems."

We did not return to Baker Street directly. Holmes requested the cabby to wait outside Scotland Yard, and vanished inside without a word. He returned shortly and we continued our journey. He spent the first few minutes peering into the passing streets ensuring, I thought, that no one followed. When he was satisfied, he spoke at last.

"Lestrade was away, Watson, but I left a message and the key. If his absence is prolonged, I expect Gregson or MacDonald will take it up."

"You are not taking an active part then, after all?"

"Oh, but I am. There is more to this than a rather clumsy attempt at persecution. I intend to discover the truth."

#

At his urging, I remained at Baker Street. When I awoke the following morning, Holmes had already gone out. The remains of his breakfast lay upon the table, and the teapot was cold. On consulting our landlady, I learned that he had left more than an hour earlier.

For me, the day passed slowly. More so, I thought, because I was anxious to learn more of the curious situation that surrounded us. I knew that Holmes would know much more, when I saw him next. At last the hour came when I could close my surgery doors. I was fortunate in finding a hansom quickly, and was soon back in my former lodgings.

I must have dozed, despite myself. A loud noise woke me and I realised that the door had been slammed below. Quick footsteps on the stairs followed, and a moment later Holmes entered the room with a flourish.

"Ah, Watson, looking distinctly better, I observe."

"I find myself less distressed, thanks to your help and advice."

He struggled out of his coat and laid his hat on a side-table. "I have much to tell you, old fellow. Let us prevail upon Mrs Hudson for coffee, after which I will reveal all."

We had finished our coffee and the tray had been retrieved by our landlady, before we sat back in our chairs and he produced his old briar. During this short interval there had been little conversation between us, and I sensed that he waited for me to calm myself of any remaining feelings of discomfort regarding the nature of this affair.

He blew a cloud of aromatic smoke into the air above him, and began:

"As you know, Watson, I have various sources of information across London. I had to visit many of these today, gleaning bits and pieces as I progressed. At the end of my enquiries I felt much as if I had spent the day retrieving pieces of a puzzle, so that only now could I see the entire picture. I must say though, that every moment spent in this pursuit was worth the effort, for now the situation is clear to me."

"I am anxious to know how Mary is connected with this."

"And so you shall. Our adversary's intention was, as I suspected, to bring about not only your death, but mine also. Nor is that the end of it, as you will see. His first step was to make it appear that your wife had returned to life, thus causing you considerable distress and probably giving rise to new hope that could have no fulfilment. I believe his aim was to make you doubt your own senses, and to upset the balance of your mind. In addition, he knew that this would have a detrimental effect on me, because we are friends. He spent considerable time in learning about our activities by consorting with the criminal classes. This was a fatal mistake, since some of those he consulted were also my informants."

I could contain myself no longer. "Who is this, Holmes? Someone, perhaps, who we have brought to grief before now?"

"That is not entirely true." He drew on his pipe for a final time, before knocking it out on the hearth. "Do you recall the last few days, before we set off for the Continent to escape Professor Moriarty?"

"I do, and they are not pleasant memories."

"Indeed. You may remember that I looked down on Baker Street from this very room, and remarked that our lodgings were under observation."

"A man called Stoker, I think you said."

"You are almost correct. It was Stuker, a professional garrotter of German extraction, and one of Moriarty's most efficient henchman."

I thought back and shook my head. "He cannot be behind this, Holmes, although that would explain the method used to murder Miss Bowman, for I recall reading in *The Standard* that he had died in prison."

"There was a younger brother, a more recent addition to Moriarty's organisation. He is thought to have left the country some time before Scotland Yard closed its net around the gang, and has not been heard of since."

"And you suspect this man intends to kill us?"

"From the information provided by my informants, I am forced to that conclusion. You were to be hounded until you doubted your own sanity, before being despatched in the manner of Miss Bowman, and I was to follow soon after. These were to be acts of revenge for Stuker's capture and subsequent demise. I have said that our deaths would not be the end of this, which is apparent when we consider that Inspector Lestrade was closely involved with the capture of the gang."

"Lestrade?" I said in astonishment. "He is to be the next victim?"

"So I have concluded, from the answers to the questions I asked of my Underworld contacts."

I rose from my chair. "We must inform him at once! He is in deadly danger."

"Calm yourself, Watson. I have reason to believe that these murders were to be carried out in rotation. It was to be first you, then me, before the good inspector. As our adversary has not yet progressed beyond causing severe distress to yourself, I do not think that Lestrade is in immediate danger, though preparations for his demise may be in hand. Regarding ourselves however, I suggest we take the greatest care until this is over. I will accompany you, when dinner is concluded, back to your home in Kensington where, if you will allow me to advise you, it would be wise for you to pack a bag with enough clean shirts and whatever else you need, to last for about a week. This may be unnecessary, but I cannot ignore the likely threat."

"You are sending me out of London?"

A quick smile crept across his features. "Much to the contrary, old fellow, I am asking you to move back here for a while. Mrs Hudson approves wholeheartedly."

"I will be glad to." A feeling of warmth and contentment swept through me, despite everything. "It will be like old times."

"Indeed. Including the early capture of our opponent, I sincerely hope."

#

That evening saw me move back to Baker Street without incident. Holmes had suggested that, while our lives were under threat, we should remain in each other's company at all times save while we slept, and I therefore made arrangements by telegraph for my practice to be temporarily in the care of a locum.

The following morning we breakfasted early and were seated in Lestrade's office before nine o'clock. We refused tea and the little detective closed the door, shutting out the protestations of a prisoner who was being marched along the corridor.

"Now then, gentlemen, I presume it is the murder of Miss Bowman that you are here to talk to me about. I can tell you that whoever did it was careful, for we have found few clues as yet. Nevertheless, he will make a slip, you mark my words, if he hasn't already. I have only just returned from Sussex, on another matter, otherwise we would doubtlessly have progressed further." He paused for a moment, before directing his gaze to my friend and asking, "Can I enquire, Mr Holmes, what it is that you have discovered, and why you and Doctor Watson visited this lady's house?"

Holmes' expression was unaltered. "To answer your questions in reverse, Lestrade, Watson and I were there in the course of an investigation in which Miss Bowman was involved. As for our discoveries, they were remarkably few because, as you have said, the killer was careful. I have, however, shed more light on this matter since then, and I can tell you without the slightest doubt that not only are our lives in danger from the same source, but yours also."

The inspector became very still for a moment. Then, to my surprise, he laughed.

"Come, Mr Holmes, this is nothing new. We are used to this sort of threat, here at the Yard. There is always some villain who wishes to get back at the force after a spell in prison." He paused, his expression changing and his eyes flitting from Holmes to me and back again. "You appear to be taking this seriously. Is there something more?"

Holmes then related the events since my encounter with the coach in the fog, and their connection with the murder of Miss Agnes Bowman. Finally, he confided his conclusions.

"We had all three better watch our steps then, Mr Holmes," Lestrade said when my friend ceased to speak, "but you need have no worries on my account. I have had a new fellow assigned to me, to learn the trade so to speak. Detective-Sergeant Cullen is a strong, reliable officer who has recently joined the force. He can serve as my bodyguard," he smiled, to indicate that this was something of a jest, "as well as learning the ropes. He volunteered to work with me, impressed by my reputation I'm sure, so now this killer of yours has to deceive two pairs of eyes instead of one. I do not think he will find it easy."

"I am certain that he will not," Holmes confirmed, "but perhaps I can request something of you."

The bulldog-like face became a mask of suspicion. "You can, Mr Holmes, but I cannot guarantee my agreement."

Holmes glanced at me and then looked at the inspector with concern. Then to my astonishment he contradicted the intentions he had previously expressed to me. "I would be obliged if you would let Doctor Watson accompany you and the detective-sergeant for, let us say, a week as you perform your official duties. I realise that this is an irregular procedure, but I have the greatest respect for the cunning and resourcefulness of the murderer of Miss Bowman. If your precautions should fail, the presence of a medical man may well be the difference that ensures the survival of yourself and others."

Lestrade looked surprised at first, even outraged at this suggestion, and for a moment I expected him to refuse absolutely. Then his expression cleared, and he smiled cynically. "That is an unusual request as you say, but I cannot see that any harm could result from it. Who knows, Mr Holmes, Doctor Watson might learn something from our way of doing things, to his advantage."

"There is that possibility, of course," Holmes said with a straight face. "Thank you, Inspector."

#

The week passed slowly. Lestrade was a methodical and persistent policeman, but appeared slow to me after Holmes. I saw my friend only at breakfast and in the evening, and he would say little of his own activities. I related to him my observations of every case where I had accompanied the inspector and Detective-Sergeant Cullen, and his invariable response was a slow nodding of his head. At no time was there any incident that could be connected with Miss Bowman's killer and, as his own investigation had halted for lack of new evidence, I believe Lestrade had dismissed the affair from his mind.

I discovered later that Holmes had followed us closely. The elderly country gentleman, the bespectacled lawyer, the plodding schoolmaster and the coarsely-spoken groom and others were all present at some stage of Lestrade's cases. All of them were different, all of them were Holmes.

As for Detective-Sergeant Robert Cullen, he seemed an agreeable fellow. Rather reticent at first, I soon discovered that he possessed a not inconsiderable knowledge of medicine, was well-informed regarding the geography of the British Isles and, like myself, had a weakness for the fair sex. He was a tall man, as much so as Holmes, but more heavily-built. He wore a sombre expression that frequently changed to a knowing smile, and I began to suspect that he was far more acquainted with the ways of the world than his manner would suggest.

By the end of the week I had become disenchanted with the task that Holmes had given me. On the afternoon of the last day he appeared at Scotland Yard, apparently pursuing a different matter since he requested an interview with Inspector Gregson. This was granted, and had not concluded as I left with Lestrade and Cullen. Later, at dinner, he dismissed the encounter lightly, and I knew that to pursue the subject would be futile.

However, he continued to follow Lestrade's activities through me. Reluctantly, I agreed to spend a further week with the inspector, who seemed already to be aware of the arrangement when I mentioned it. I formed the impression that some change had taken place, that the situation had become more urgent, since three constables were unexpectedly added to our group. Constable Cheshire was a slow but purposeful middle-aged man who spoke unceasingly about his family. Constable Harbridge was tall and brisk, with a magnificent handlebar moustache and Constable Curtis was short and bald with a fixed, determined expression that never varied. As the days progressed, I was no longer able to pick out individuals who might be Holmes in disguise, and I therefore concluded that he watched us from concealment.

There continued to be no incident that could be construed as an attempt on Lestrade's life, and it occurred to me that Stuker's younger brother, if indeed it was he, might be allowing us to develop a false sense of security, while he awaited his opportunity to strike. This apparent halt in the case began to concern me, as did Holmes' seemingly declining interest. I had seen little of my friend of late, when I was in our rooms he was elsewhere, and vice-versa.

I had watched Lestrade even more carefully, during this second week spent in his company. He had solved a burglary case and apprehended a young man who sustained himself by robbing elderly ladies, and rightly commented that he considered himself to have done well. On the last day occurred the events that I had long expected, but dreaded.

Dusk was closing in rapidly when Detective-Sergeant Cullen burst into Lestrade's office with the news that a report had been received of a sighting of George Mellor in the grounds of a house in Clapham Common. George Mellor was wanted for at least three murders, and it had long been Lestrade's ambition to capture him because, among other reasons, his colleague Mr Peter Jones had attempted to do so and failed.

By the time we reached Suttliffe Court, for so the place was called, full darkness had fallen. Our party comprised Lestrade, Cullen, the three constables and myself. We travelled in two police wagons and the inspector ordered the drivers to take their conveyances to the end of the quiet tree-lined street to await our return. A rusty gate set in a long high wall allowed us admittance, and we found ourselves in a small wood with the house a short distance beyond.

"The house has been unoccupied for some time," Lestrade said. "The owner died leaving no heir. Mellor may be hiding inside or among the trees. Do not use your lanterns, lest he become aware of our approach, and proceed silently. Spread out across the forest, and move in a line forwards. We should reach the courtyard soon."

"I will search in this direction, with Doctor Watson." Detective-Sergeant Cullen whispered somewhat surprisingly. Lestrade murmured his assent and he and the others melted into the darkness. I peered around me, to see only the vague outlines of bare branches. Nowhere was there a glimmer of light.

"This way, Doctor." Cullen moved confidently forward and I followed, guided by the faint sounds of his passage rather than sight. We seemed to progress in a sideways direction. Possibly his intention was to approach the house from a different direction to the others, cutting off another route by which Mellor might escape. We emerged into a tiny clearing and he stopped suddenly.

"Have you seen something?" I asked in a low voice.

To my surprise, a vesta flared suddenly. By its light I could make out the revolver that Cullen had pointed in my direction. He blew out the flame, and we were again in darkness.

"Do not move," he said in a different voice. "Come no closer."

74

"What is happening?"

"You are about to witness the culmination of much planning, Watson. That is why Lestrade and yourself are here."

An awful realisation came to me. Fear held me in a tight grip.

"George Mellor's presence was a fabrication, I presume."

"An invention of mine. I knew that Lestrade's ambition would compel him to attend here immediately. The setting is perfect."

"For what purpose, exactly?" But I knew the answer, already.

He laughed. An eerie sound. "I do believe that Detective-Sergeant Cullen, an acquaintance who I cultivated purposefully, asked me a similar question, before I killed him. Also Miss Bowman, I think."

"Then you are....." I began.

"Jonathan Stuker," he finished. "I am sure your friend Mr Holmes has deduced that, by now. He may also have realised the reason for my actions. Together with you and Lestrade, and others who I have yet to identify, he was the cause of the death of my brother. I could not let that pass, without setting myself upon a path of vengeance."

"Your brother was a murderer. Had that been proven, he would have died on the gallows."

"I prefer to think of him as one who chose a different way through life, as did his employer Professor Moriarty, and as did I. All of the hunting class, you see, the slaughterers of those who obstruct us."

"Why did you bring my deceased wife into this?"

He was silent for a moment, during which I listened in vain for sounds of the others among the trees.

"My original plan was to make both you and Holmes suffer," he said then. "You, because I was certain that you had not fully recovered from her death, and he as your close friend. Had this been successful, you would have known much pain and confusion before you met the fate I had in store for you. Mr Holmes I intended to deal with later, and Lestrade after that. I regret that my strategy had less than the desired effect, but we are here now and Lestrade will meet the same fate as you are about to, before I slip away. By this time tomorrow I will be far from here, and Scotland Yard will be short of one Detective-Sergeant." I sensed a movement, and concluded that he had pulled something from his pocket. "It is fitting that you should receive the death that my brother was so adept at bestowing. Turn around."

With his revolver trained on me, I had no choice but to obey. Already, I imagined the sharpness of the wire that he had drawn from his pocket, cutting into my throat and extinguishing my life. Fear I felt, yes, even terror, but even greater was the dreadful thought that I was unable to warn Holmes of what was to befall him. I had some notion of turning to face Stuker as he approached, to grapple with him in a desperate bid to survive, but this was dashed as he was behind me so rapidly and I heard the wire hiss as he swung it over my head.

It began to tighten, but before it could sink into my flesh I sensed a quick movement from the nearest trees. I turned my head as the vague form of Constable Harbridge dealt a blow to Stuker, his truncheon striking not the head but the hands that gripped the wire. I heard the breaking of bone, before the resulting cry of agony became lost in the forest.

I carefully unwound the wire from my neck, and threw the vile thing to the leaf-strewn earth.

"Thank you, Constable," I gasped inadequately, turning to the indistinct shape. "You appeared at just the right moment. An instant more, and I would have been a dead man."

"You surely cannot believe that I would have allowed that, Watson, after listening to Stuker's confession."

"Holmes!" I cried in astonishment, as I recognized his voice.

I detected movement as he removed the moustache. "It is gratifying to see that I can surprise you, after all these years. Are you injured, old fellow?"

"Not at all, you prevented that. But how did you know to follow us?"

I sensed his smile, in the gloom. "You will recall that I was at Scotland Yard when 'Cullen' was introduced to us. When he removed his gloves I noticed at once the marks across his hands where he had encircled the wire around them to take the strain as he murdered Miss Bowman. The marks were fresh but far from conclusive and without proof I could do nothing, hence my successful attempt to persuade Gregson to allow 'Constable Harbridge' to temporarily join the force. I explained that both yourself and Lestrade were in deadly danger, and he eventually agreed after impressing upon me many times that I was engaging in a most irregular procedure. I think my past assistance to The Yard swayed his final decision."

Stuker let out a long moan as Holmes lit a lantern and handed it to me. "Let us make our way back to the road, where Lestrade and the others will be waiting. I informed them of the truth of this matter before I left to follow you." He then gripped our prisoner by the arm, with more force than I had seen him use before and disregarding his injuries. Stuker appeared to move with great difficulty, but this was disregarded. Not long after, he was transferred to the custody of Inspector Lestrade, and my friend and

I engaged a passing four-wheeler to return to Baker Street. A short while later we were sitting comfortably in our familiar armchairs, he having resumed his normal appearance. Before a warming fire, we sipped glasses of an excellent port.

"I am glad that this business is concluded, Watson," he said as he put down his glass, "if only to see the relief to you that comes from exposing the false resurrection of your wife. Although you knew, as I have always been convinced, that such a thing is impossible, the immense emotional shock to you was evident. I cannot apologise enough for my insensitivity to your predicament."

I shook my head. "Much to the contrary, your voice of reason helped me to retain my senses. It does prove however, that Mary's death still affects me more than I had realised."

"We all need time to heal, old fellow. Some of us more than others." He was silent for a moment, before retrieving his glass and draining it. "I think it best if we strive to put this affair behind us. If, as you have indicated, you wish to move back into your old room, I suggest you occupy yourself tomorrow with transferring your remaining possessions from Kensington. As for now, I think we have both earned a good night's rest."

With that he stood up and stretched himself before bidding me goodnight, and a moment later I was alone in our sitting-room. Shortly after I sank gratefully into my bed, weary enough to expect a dreamless sleep. In fact my dreams were vivid and very real to me. They were of Mary, clad in a long white gown, calling to me in the sweet voice that I could never forget. She told me that she knew of the strain of my recent experience and should disregard it for the falsity it had been. Reassuringly, she said that she was and always would be with me still, and would watch over me. She spoke of a sign that she would leave for me, but I knew not her meaning.

I awoke to a new day with sunlight filling the room. The dream had been curiously uplifting, though of course it was nothing more than a wishful product of my imagination. I decided not to mention it to Holmes, in order to avoid bringing down upon me another lecture of the folly of believing in the supernatural or anything that could be construed to be connected with it.

Our breakfast conversation was pleasant enough, my friend eager to embark upon the new case he had referred to before. He left early and I returned to my house in Kensington, later that morning. I walked around the familiar rooms, allowing memories to return to me briefly. The cart I had engaged waited outside with the horse stamping its hooves impatiently, and two burly young fellows stood ready to enter and begin removing my possessions. I was about to call for this to begin when I hesitated, having noticed a strange thing: my slippers, my pipe and the book I was in the midst of reading were arranged as she would have done, as she used to do. I had no memory of doing this when I was here last, and surely Holmes would have made some comment had I mentioned it. I resolved to say nothing of this to him, but in my mind, and indeed my heart, the conclusion was clear.

## The Adventure of Miss Anna Truegrace

Despite the continuing rain, I had decided on a short walk after breakfast. Sherlock Holmes was in the blackest of moods, hardly consenting even to acknowledge my greeting as I emerged from my room, and causing me to seek the open air in order to steel myself against his morose demeanour. I had taken a few days away from my practice, which a young locum had enthusiastically taken over, in order to settle some legal matters concerning my late wife. These had been concluded unexpectedly speedily, and I had hoped to spend my remaining free time assisting my friend on some new case, but none had as yet presented itself to disperse his dark disposition. After walking the wet pavements for half an hour I resolved to return to Baker Street, and it was as I approached our lodgings that I saw two people beneath a large umbrella standing uncertainly nearby. Folding down and shaking my own umbrella, I opened the door and stepped inside, before turning to face the couple. It was indeed a man and a woman as I had supposed.

"Mr Sherlock Holmes?" the man enquired.

"No, but this is his residence. I am his associate, Doctor John Watson, and I am sure Mr Holmes will see you. Please leave your umbrella in the hallstand there, and follow me."

They did so, the lady closing the front door before they climbed the stairs behind me. I stepped into our sitting room with something of a flourish, watching with relief and pleasure my friend's surprise on seeing that I was accompanied.

"Ah, Watson. You have bought me new clients, I perceive."

"Conceivably, though I have not yet enquired as to their difficulty."

Holmes smiled quickly and introduced himself, having shed his rueful expression. "I have high hopes that they will present me with an interesting problem. I saw them alight from a four-wheeler as I looked down from our window, and noted that it took fully four minutes of discussion before they decided to approach our door. Surely, a simple matter would have required less consultation." He gestured towards the armchairs near the fire. "Pray let Doctor Watson relieve you of your outer garments and come to sit near the fire while I call for tea. Then, when you are ready, you can explain to me how I can assist you."

I saw relief in the faces of both our visitors as I hung up their coats. Holmes shouted down to Mrs Hudson and closed the door, before we took our seats.

"I am Mr Cedric Truegrace," the young man began rather stiffly before either Holmes or I could speak, "and this is my sister Miss Anna Truegrace."

"You work in a clerical capacity and your sister has great fear of you," Holmes finished.

Mr Truegrace appeared shocked. I had seen Holmes perform this feat many times before, but on this occasion it held no mystery for me. Our visitors glanced at each other, astonishment written on their faces.

"How in the world…."

"Come now, Mr Truegrace," my friend continued. "The ink on your shirt cuff tells its own story, also revealing that you are left-handed, and anxious glances from your sister have been directed at you since the moment you entered the room." His stare grew hard. "Do you beat this lady, sir?"

I half-rose from my chair, horrified at the prospect of this innocent-looking girl being subjected to such treatment.

"No, gentlemen," she said quickly. "That is not the situation at all."

"I swear that I would never do any such thing," her brother protested. As he spoke I heard the rattle of teacups outside our door and immediately intercepted Mrs Hudson to relieve her of the tray. I placed it on a side-table and poured for the four of us, before Mr Truegrace continued. "No, things have occurred differently. It is a strange story."

"We are quite used to those." Holmes assured him.

"Anna saw herself in a vision, as the victim of a murderer. She could not see his face, but heard herself call my name."

Holmes surprised me by not receiving this with incredulity. He looked at Miss Truegrace with a thoughtful expression on his face. "You could not be mistaken? For example, could it be that you were calling to your brother for assistance?"

"Truly, I cannot say, for the vision was no more than a blurred image. I only know that I have been in mortal terror since. It is only with the greatest effort that I can bear to be in the company of Cedric, such is the pain of my apprehension."

The next few moments were passed in silence as we drank. It came to me that this account might be suitable for the eyes of my publisher, with Holmes' permission, and so I spent the interval in observing our visitors' appearance.

Mr Truegrace, I believed, was in his late twenties, while his sister was perhaps two years his junior. They were of average height, he with dark whiskers along his jawbone and almost reaching his chin, while her auburn tresses hung shining below her bonnet. From their speech, I formed the impression that their education had not been neglected.

Miss Truegrace spoke again suddenly. "Such things have happened to me before, over the years, but never like this. That Cedric would harm me I cannot believe, and yet it is what I saw."

At once disappointment crept into my friend's face, yet I also sensed that he was mildly amused. He had anticipated a confrontation with a problem of complexity or intrigue, only to be faced with what he would surely regard as little more than a fairy story.

"I have encountered a 'visionary' before," Holmes said in a slow voice of forced tolerance. "I accompanied a client of a few years ago to a meeting, where a woman who called herself 'The Enlightened One' would retire to a locked room and experience visions with messages for members of her audience without. She appeared to be remarkably successful and profited greatly, until I discovered that another onlooker left the chamber at the same time with the selection of each new subject. He turned out to be her accomplice, who disclosed to her information he had gleaned through overheard conversations while mingling with the spectators, communicated through a parallel window by mirror flashes using a pre-arranged code." He fixed our visitors with a stern gaze. "You will see then, why I find the concept incredible, even humorous, in its way."

"Was this during your residence in Montague Street?" I asked, not having heard this account before.

"It was well before your time, Watson. I had almost forgotten the affair. It was a ridiculously simple matter, which I solved quite quickly. The woman's stipulation that she was open to these experiences only on fine days, gave it away at once."

"My experiences are not rooted in trickery!' Miss Truegrace retorted. "They have troubled me all of my life."

"She speaks the truth," her brother confirmed. "There have been many instances during our childhood when such happenings have caused her distress, especially when our parents and other adults in whom she placed her confidence humoured her or responded with mockery. She informed a neighbour that his horse would run off, never to be seen again, and that very thing occurred within a week. A child disappeared and was found alive and well, exactly as Anna had described. As with all the other instances, her ability was never acknowledged."

"And recently? I cannot think that you would be here today, were there nothing more."

"There is indeed, Mr Holmes. Two weeks ago our elderly maid, Ellen, collapsed and died while in our village on an errand. Four days before, Anna told me that this would happen. We confided in no one, not wishing to attract again the ridicule of years before. One of the reasons that we gave up our home in the centre of Worcester to  move to Courtney Dale, was to escape this."

"And when did your latest experience occur?"

"This morning," Miss Truegrace said in a subdued voice. "During the early hours."

"But no crime has actually been committed?"

Her brother looked suddenly uncomfortable. "None, which is why we cannot avail ourselves of the protection of the official force. We have heard however, that you specialise in throwing light on the inexplicable."

"I have said before that I have no belief in the supernatural, and you must surely realise that even if that were not so and such things were a reality, I would have no power against them. Perhaps a priest would be of more use to you than I."

There was a long silence, during which our visitors took on a look of despair. Doubtlessly, I reflected, Sherlock Holmes was their last hope of preventing a crime that had yet to happen. I reviewed the words of Mr Truegrace, and the fate of the maid, Ellen, troubled me. An incident from long ago came into my mind.

"Holmes, I have to tell you that I, also, have met something like this before." He turned his head towards me, as I continued. "I once had a patient, a most down-to-earth young woman whose honesty I would have staked my life upon, who often professed to have visions. She also had some success with her predictions, although she never attempted to profit from them. Neither were any of her revelations harmful."

From his expression, I saw that my interruption had not been welcomed. It was clear to me, because I knew my friend, that a conflict was raging in his mind. Despite his rejection of the mystical, he was reluctant to return to the stagnation that had been upon him before the appearance of this curious affair.

A succession of hansoms passed along Baker Street as he collected his thoughts. The cries of the coachmen, urging their horses to greater speed, and the occasional crack of a whip floated up to us through the half-open window. The hiss of metal-rimmed wheels on the wet road surface told me that the rain had resumed.

"I will look into this," Holmes said then, "but not from a supernatural aspect. I accept that you, Miss Truegrace, could possess an ability that we do not fully understand. The demise of your maid gives an element of truth to your fears, and if I can prevent you suffering the fate that you have witnessed then I am bound to do so. Tell me, was Ellen's death accepted as by natural causes?"

"Doctor Caulfield examined her thoroughly. The death certificate states that she died from heart failure, and we have since discovered that she had a history of such an affliction."

"No doubt she failed to inform you of this for fear of losing her position," I ventured. "Although I am sure she need not have feared on that score."

Mr Truegrace nodded. "Not at all. She served us well."

"I take it that you are employed within the village, Mr Truegrace." Holmes enquired.

"As you correctly deduced, I earn my living as a clerk. I work for our local solicitors, Craven & Hibberdson. Mr Craven has been dead for some years, but the name has been retained. There is just Mr Fyffe Hibberdson and myself, and a secretary that attends when required."

"I take it that you reside not far away."

"Tregothan Farm, the name by which it is still called although it has not functioned as such for many years, is situated about a half mile further on from the village of Courtney Dale. It is not difficult to find, since the drive leads directly from the main Worcester Road."

Holmes nodded. "The local inns provide fair accommodation, I trust."

"Most certainly. There are several of good reputation."

"Excellent." My friend rose and we all did the same. "I do not think that there is much else that I need to know, at this point. You may expect us on the early afternoon train tomorrow. We will visit you at your residence after some preliminary enquiries. Also," he looked directly at Miss Truegrace, "I would reassure you as to your brother's intentions. There can be no doubt that something is amiss here, or that some crime has been committed or will be committed, but the perpetrator will, I am sure, not be he. We will see what comes of a few enquiries thereabouts."

Our visitors then thanked us both and left.

"What was it that convinced you of Mr Truegrace's lack of malice towards his sister?" I asked Holmes as we watched from our window our clients hailing a cab.

"Did you not see the pain in his eyes as she recounted the vision and her interpretation of it?" He shook his head. "No man could manufacture such deep grief as the accusation caused him."

"I confess that I did not, but I detected a tremor in his voice."

He took his Bradshaw from the bookshelf. "Watson, have you sufficient time left before resuming your practice, to accompany me on a brief visit to Worcestershire?"

"You do not anticipate a lengthy investigation, then?"

"I believe I have assimilated a fair idea of what we may be dealing with here. I find this result disturbing though, as I am at a loss to explain Miss Truegrace's vision. There are, however, several gaps in my understanding of the likely sequence of events. We will clear those up in a day or two, I think."

"I am with you, Holmes, as ever."

"I thought I knew my Watson," he smiled.

#

The following morning found us at Paddington Station in time for the early train. I recall little of the journey, other than Holmes' observations concerning the countryside and, occasionally, of the waiting passengers at the various stations through which we passed. Eventually he lapsed into silence as he became lost in his own thoughts, and I think I would have fallen asleep had he not suddenly peered through the window as the train came to a halt.

"We have arrived I think, Watson. This is Shrub Hill Station."

We retrieved our scant luggage and were among the first to alight. No trap or cart awaited us, but Holmes quickly selected and engaged a burly, red-haired fellow from the half-dozen drivers who lined the platform. We learned that Courtney Dale was three miles distant, and Tregothan Farm a further half mile.

We passed through leafy countryside, fresh from recent rains, and a lake in a field of uncut grass before the straight road led us to Courtney Dale. The village appeared to comprise mostly of the shops along this thoroughfare, which began and ended with a church of striking architecture. I noticed that several side-streets branched off to our left, some containing warehouses and further trading establishments while others boasted long rows of villas of local stone. Holmes instructed our driver to halt as he caught sight of an inn of impressive appearance, and proceeded to carry both his bag and my own through its door. He returned within ten minutes.

"I have secured us two good, clean rooms," he informed me, "and in deference to you I have ascertained that the cuisine is quite edible."

"Thank you for your consideration."

"But now," he said, standing beside the cart, "I think we should explore this charming village before we go about our business. I will pay this good fellow what we owe and we can visit Tregothan Farm later."

After we had watched our driver turn his cart around and set off back to the town, I asked my friend about his sudden change of objective.

"I noticed the office of the solicitors, Craven & Hibberdson, a short way along the street," he replied, "and thought it as well to interview Mr Fyffe Hibberdson, if he is available, immediately as a possible way to bring this enquiry to a more speedy conclusion."

#

We sat opposite the solicitor, across his desk, in a wood-panelled office that smelled faintly of cigar-smoke.

Mr Fyffe Hibberdson had little of the appearance that one associates with members of his profession. From above the spotless winged collar a weather-beaten face, such as old sailors often have, held a critical expression. He was of no more than average height, but of stocky build with thick hair that was prematurely grey. I would have placed him as about thirty-five years of age but his gaze was of one much older. Probably, I concluded, as a result of much time spent unravelling the legal problems of others.

"I have heard much about you, Mr Holmes," he said with surprising friendliness, "not least from the most entertaining accounts of Doctor Watson, here."

"I am glad that you find them interesting," I said.

"Indeed I do," he smiled. "But tell me, what has brought you to this office, today?"

Holmes answered before I could speak. "I am conducting an enquiry in which someone of your acquaintance is loosely concerned. It is not a serious matter, but it is always as well to learn something of those on the fringe of the situation in order to obtain a more complete appreciation of the circumstances. Knowing of your connection, it occurred to me that you might be prepared to furnish some basic information."

"I understand." Something of what might have been relief crossed Mr Hibberdson's face. "I will, of course, help if I can. That is to say, provided than no aspect of confidentiality is breached."

"Capital. I understand that you have in your employment Mr Cedric Truegrace."

"My clerk? It is he that you wish to enquire about?"

"To be more precise, it is his sister. Presumably you will have met her on social occasions, or perhaps she has called here from time to time."

Mr Hibberdson nodded. "That is so. They were among my guests for an informal evening, no more than two weeks past. I had met her previously of course, and I must confess that she struck me as, how shall I put it, a rather nervous girl. She appeared to me as the sort of person who is powerless to prevent her imagination running away with her, so to speak."

"As a medical man, I can confirm that," I commented, more as an encouragement of him to elaborate than from my observations.

"What, in particular, caused you to draw such a conclusion?" Holmes asked Mr Hibberdson.

"I am uncertain, after all I am a solicitor and not a doctor, but probably it was my impression that she was possessed of a state of constant unease. As I have said, I am totally unqualified to judge, but I sensed that she is to some extent neurotic or even in the grip of the early stages of brain fever."

"An extensive diagnosis, nevertheless," I observed.

"Not as such," Mr Hibberdson's expression lightened. "I say this only because I have seen similar symptoms in others, before now."

Holmes rose to his feet, and I did the same. "You have been most helpful, Mr Hibberdson, in enhancing my investigation. I will now wish you good day sir, with my thanks."

The solicitor accompanied us to the door and showed us out courteously. As we left I noticed that his eyes now held a quite different expression, perhaps a hint of uncertainty or fear. It crossed my mind that, should this affair conclude with Mr Cedric Truegrace facing some sort of criminal charges after all, then a replacement clerk might, in a country village, be difficult to come by. This possibility, I imagined, would cause a degree of concern to Mr Hibberdson.

#

After a scant lunch in a nearby tea-house we secured one of the few hansoms in the village, all of which were operated by a single company, for the half-mile to Tregothan Farm. The outhouses spread across the wide yard revealed at once the previous purpose of the place, before Mr Truegrace and his sister adopted it as their residence. I had imagined it to boast a thatched roof, but in fact the house was adorned with purple slate. The walls, I could see, were once white, but now a creeping green moss discoloured the upper floors. As our conveyance left us, Holmes strode to the door with me in his wake. It opened before he could knock, and Miss Anna Truegrace admitted us.

We were conducted to a tastefully-decorated parlour, where Mr Cedric Truegrace rose from his armchair as we entered. Greetings were exchanged and glasses of sherry bought and consumed, before our host cautiously asked whether our enquiries had yet yielded anything of significance.

"It would be true to say that I have made some progress," Holmes answered.

"From what source?" Mr Truegrace asked.

"Less than an hour ago I interviewed your employer, Mr Fyffe Hibberdson."

Our host's uncertain expression deepened. "But how is he involved in this?"

"He is not, as yet. He has provided information about the general situation here, which I consider essential if I am to arrive at the solution to this most unusual case. I must now make of you a request, to the same end."

"What is it that you wish?" Miss Truegrace enquired.

My friend turned in his chair, so that he faced them both. "I would like you to conduct me on a tour of this house, especially the room where you experienced the 'vision'."

Mr Truegrace sprang to his feet instantly. "That is a condition which is easily satisfied." He beckoned in a way that encompassed both Holmes and myself. "Come."

We followed him throughout the building, Holmes making examinations of the walls in all rooms. There seemed nothing remarkable anywhere, but he ensured most of all that the room of Miss Gracechurch's experience, the master bedroom, was sound.

"Well, Mr Holmes," our host said when we were all settled again, "can I take it that you discovered something that will throw some light on the situation?"

"You may take it that I found exactly what I expected to find."

"And what is that, pray?"

"I found nothing. That is to say that I found nothing to either substantiate or dismiss the theory that I have formed."

"How disappointing," Miss Truegrace commented.

"May I ask how long it is since you took up residence here," I asked.

Mr Truegrace considered for a moment. "Why, it must be almost three years, by now. We hoped the change would somehow see an end to Anna's visions."

"Was the experience concerning the maid the first since then?" Holmes enquired.

"It was. Until that occurrence we believed we had been successful in leaving them behind."

"Can you recall from whom you bought the property?"

"I cannot, but that information is easily obtainable. The papers are in my study."

He made to rise, but his sister precluded the action. "There is no need, Cedric. I remember that the previous owner was Mr Gareth Sternwell. He had lived here but a short while, when an inheritance enabled him to move to grander accommodation on the far side of the village. I believe that he mentioned his former profession to be that of a professional gambler, in Worcester."

"Most interesting," Holmes remarked.

"Mr Holmes, are we not clutching at straws here," Mr Truegrace asked in a puzzled voice. "After all, it was the strange vision and the resulting dread of my sister that drove us to consult you. I do not see how our history can reveal anything."

My friend regarded him with an expression that gave away nothing. After a moment of silence he spoke quietly. "Due to the singular nature of this case, for it is one the like of which I have not had placed before me until now, I must approach it in a befitting fashion. From the first I had formulated several theories, most of which have been disproved by subsequent events, but I am determined to establish whether your sister's vision, as you refer to it, has any substance or is merely fanciful. Be content to let me proceed in my own way, humour me if you will, for I have high expectations that the truth of this matter will be evident before long." He rose and picked up his hat. "But as for now, I think a late afternoon walk back to the village will provide sufficient stimulation for me to consider at length the information that you have furnished. Come, Watson."

We left Tregothan Farm then, I with the feeling that Holmes considered himself the subject of a mild insult. He was silent, staring at the grassy slope underfoot, as we walked parallel to the road for much of the way. Only once did he vary his posture, glancing suddenly towards a group of trees while a hansom and two four-wheelers passed us as if he suspected that we were observed, before we came upon the outskirts of the village and then the inn. After changing our clothes we enjoyed an excellent meal of roast pork, and then spent some time in conversation over pints of good ale before retiring a little earlier than was our custom.

#

At breakfast, Holmes asked the landlord about the whereabouts of Mr Gareth Sternwell. Having served us bacon, eggs and toast, the fellow scratched his head before the answer came to him.

"Ah, I know who you mean sir, now that I've thought about it. He was a gambler or a betting man in Worcester, I think. These days he lives in a place called Parkfield Heights, on a hill leading out of the village as you pass the old miller's pond and the livery stable. I'm told the house looks like as Greek temple, so you can't miss it. Most of the gamblers I've known end up as beggars, but this one must have done well for himself, wouldn't you say?"

"Indeed, it would seem so," Holmes acknowledged. "My thanks to you, landlord."

Shortly afterwards we were fortunate in procuring a hansom that had dropped its fare at the inn as we were about to leave. It left us near the brow of a hill covered in tall elms and flowering shrubs, within sight of a structure that did indeed resemble the abode of the Olympian gods.

"This man surely did well at the tables," I remarked.

Holmes opened the wrought iron gate to allow us to pass onto the steep drive. "Possibly, but from the description of our clients I would say that his inheritance most likely determined his future."

We were rather breathless after the short climb. Holmes lifted the heavy door-knocker, shaped like the head of a tiger, and released it. The impact echoed among the pillars that stood to each side of us, before a liveried footman opened the door and asked us our business. Holmes produced his card and we waited until the fellow returned. With a little bow, he informed us that Mr Sternwell would see us in the breakfast room.

I confess to being overawed by the splendour of the place. Mr Sternwell must have inherited a vast sum, I thought, to possess such a home. The footman led us along a short corridor, into a large airy room that reminded me of a hothouse such as tropical plants require to flourish in our country. I saw aspidistras and tall flowers, surrounding a large table on which the remains of a meal awaited removal. A short distance away stood several armchairs, upholstered in a garish pattern, and a matching settee where a man lounged as he watched us.

"Good morning, gentlemen," he said without rising. "Tell me, what possible reason could there be for me to receive a visit from a consulting detective? I assure you, my gambling debts have long since been settled."

We returned his greeting. I could tell that Holmes was slightly put out by the man's lack of courtesy. Mr Sternwell struck me as rather eccentric, reclining in a turquoise-patterned dressing gown as the time approached mid-morning. His thin face bore a moustache as red as his hair, and his eyes were filled with suspicion as much as any I have ever seen. I could well imagine facing his shifty gaze across a spinning roulette wheel or in the midst of a hand of chemin-de-fer.

"I see that you are anxious," Holmes observed. "Pray calm yourself, for we are not the official force and have no interest in your past activities."

Mr Sternwell adjusted his position. "I was curious as to your intentions, that is why you were admitted."

"We are here merely to ask questions, if you will permit us, concerning your previous ownership of Tregothan Farm," I enlightened him.

"Ah, that place," the wariness left his expression at once. "I lived there for but a short while, it could not have been more than a month or two, before this place became vacant and I was able to purchase it. I fear that I can tell you little about my former home, I found it to be rather uninteresting. The country life, I think, is not for me."

"We have been aware of some unusual happenings there," Holmes said. "The current owners are quite alarmed."

"Happenings? Ghosts, do you mean? Hauntings? I saw or heard not the slightest suggestion of such occurrences at any time. Look, Mr Holmes, if your clients are set on getting their money back from me, you can tell them that I won't have it! I did warn them, when they approached me to buy, that the place was old. They should have taken notice."

"That is not the case at all. They have no desire to live elsewhere, or to relinquish their home. It is simply that strange, or seemingly strange events have caused some confusion which I am attempting to clear up."

Mr Sternwell nodded. "Then I repeat, I cannot assist you."

Holmes bent his thin frame in a slight bow. "You have already done so, sir. I thank you for seeing us."

We turned and moved towards the door, where the footman had appeared, apparently without being summoned. Just as we passed a tall flowering plant that clung to the wall, Mr Sternwell called to us.

"I am sure that the man I bought the farm from would have been bound to mention anything out of the ordinary in the house. Mr Fyffe Hibberdson is an honourable man."

"You bought the farm from him? The solicitor?" Holmes turned and retraced his steps.

"I did. After his wife disappeared he seemed to be eager to change his residence. Probably he wished to be rid of unpleasant memories." He leaned forward in a conspiratorial fashion. "There were rumours, you see. It was said that she was seen around the village with Albert Ridden. Very indiscreet I'm sure, but she couldn't hope for secrecy – the walls in Courtney Dale have eyes."

"Was Mr Hibberdson aware of this?"

"Who knows? If he had become so, I doubt if his behaviour towards her would have changed. It is well-known that he took much pleasure in beating the poor woman, long before then."

"She disappeared, I think you said?"

Mr Sternwell shrugged. "So it is assumed. One morning Mr Hibberdson reported that his wife had been away all night, and expressed deep concern. Inspector Carew of the local force interviewed Albert Ridden, who seemed as puzzled as anyone else. Enquiries were made as far away as Worcester, without result, after the farms and woods hereabouts had been thoroughly searched. As I understand it Ridden was suspected for a while, until the case was abandoned because of lack of evidence."

"What was the official verdict?" Holmes enquired.

"It came to be believed that Elizabeth Hibberdson had grown weary of her situation here and left to make a new start in life. There was once some talk of her being seen as far away as Bristol, but the description was so vague that no one took it seriously."

"Most interesting. If I may trouble you once more, pray tell me about this man Albert Ridden."

Mr Sternwell lay back on well-stuffed cushions, as if the effort of these revelations had been too much for him. "In truth, I have never met the man, so I can say little other than what is considered common knowledge."

"Nevertheless, please continue."

"According to local gossip, he was always something of a tearaway. Elizabeth Hibberdson was not his first conquest by far. At the time he was employed as a labourer at Elleston Farm, five miles or so north of the village, but he suffered some sort of injury and now lives in the alms houses along Cardinal Way. I think there is no more that I can tell you, Mr Holmes. As I said, I have never set eyes on Ridden."

"Again, my thanks to you, sir," my friend said. "You have been of immense help, after all."

#

Having taken our leave, we set off down the hill. By the time we regained the inn we had become breathless and a little weary. The landlord had already begun to serve luncheon and I had no hesitation in ordering a portion of what turned out to be an excellent fish pie, while Holmes would take only a small amount of bread and cheese.

We were surprised when the landlord served wine.

"My good sir, we did not order this," Holmes remarked.

"It was delivered by a boy who is not known to me," the fellow replied. He searched in a pocket of his apron. "It was accompanied by this card."

My friend glanced at it before showing it to me: *From a grateful client.*

"From Mr Truegrace and his sister," I concluded.

"I think not. At no time did we inform them as to where we are staying."

"Who, then?"

Holmes scrutinized the bottle carefully, before pouring some of the contents into a glass. He swirled the liquid around. Smelled it and observed the sheen that had formed upon the surface.

"Landlord, there has been some negligence here. This wine, I can tell you for a certainty, was exposed to the air too soon. Pray dispose of it, but on no account let anyone drink, since the result would doubtlessly be a severe illness of the stomach."

The astonished man removed the bottle and glasses and withdrew.

"A pity, Holmes," I said. "A glass would have been welcome, before we set out."

He glanced at me with an amused expression. "I doubt you would have enjoyed it for long, Watson. I wished to avoid alarming our friend the landlord, but unless I am much mistaken it was laced with a deadly poison, probably arsenic."

"Good heavens! Who would do this?"

"We will discover that soon, I think."

Afterwards, my friend again consulted the landlord regarding local knowledge, to discover that Cardinal Way was within easy walking distance. We set off soon after.

"It is the next street on the right," I said as we strode past the Post Office, "if the landlord is to be relied upon."

"I have no doubt that he is," Holmes replied, "for I can see the sign already."

"Why are we seeking out this man Ridden, Holmes. What has he to do with the vision experienced by Miss Anna Truegrace?"

"Unless I am mistaken, this case has taken a different path, quite unlike its apparent nature at the outset. At the root of it is a very real crime."

He said no more until we were confronted by a row of identical brick terraced houses, in a long and narrow street. These, I knew, were inhabited by people who were, for various reasons, unable to support themselves. They were maintained by charitable donations, and tenants were expected to do what work they were able towards their upkeep.

Holmes rapped upon the first door with his cane. He bowed courteously to the elderly lady who answered his summons and asked if she knew the address of Albert Ridden. She nodded and pointed further along the street, giving elaborate directions. He thanked her and we continued for perhaps fifty yards, until we came upon a wide arch which we entered. After a sloping path with high walls, we found ourselves in an enclosure. I saw a small patch of ground to the right, evidently used for growing vegetables, with a small brick structure nearer to the path. Its door hung open to reveal a deep copper bowl set atop a low wall, which I presumed was for the communal washing of clothes. To our left were three houses, two with drawn curtains, and no sign of life. Holmes approached the third and again rapped with his cane.

At first there was no response, and Holmes was about to repeat his action when we heard trudging footsteps from within. The door opened, barely an inch.

"Who is it?" A hoarse voice, no more than a whisper.

"My name is Sherlock Holmes. My friend is Doctor John Watson."

"What do you want?"

"I am a consulting detective. I wish to speak to you concerning Mrs Elizabeth Hibberdson."

After a long silence, there came a breathless croak. "She is gone."

"That is why I am here."

"She disappeared. No one knows where."

Holmes paused, as if deciding how to proceed, then: "My investigation has brought me close to discovering the truth. I am hoping you will assist me."

"That is unlikely. What can I tell you?"

Mr Ridden, let me make it clear that I know what transpired between you and this lady. I am not here to judge you or Mrs Hibberdson, only to bring her murderer to justice."

The door opened a few inches wider. "You are certain that she was murdered, then?"

"I am in no doubt of it."

There was silence again for some moments, before a faint murmur. "You had better come in."

The door swung fully open and the meagre light from within framed a slightly stooped figure. As we entered, the man's features were revealed to us and I sensed Holmes grow tense, as I fought to prevent myself from recoiling with horror and revulsion.

Mr Ridden's face was distorted. Along the left side of his head was a wrinkled brown patch that ran from above the ear, past the jawbone and across part of the throat. The affected eye seemed to be set deeper than its companion, and was covered with a milky sheen. I understood at once his reason for living behind closed curtains: he wished to spare the world from the sight of him.

"We will not disturb you for long," Holmes assured him.

Mr Ridden gestured that we should sit down on the worn armchairs. "That is unimportant, sirs. I see few people these days. If I can throw any light on the fate of Elizabeth, I will be pleased to do so."

"You no longer work at Elleston farm," I presumed, "because of your injuries?"

He shook his head. "I cannot work, although God knows I have tried. What you see of me is but part of the burden I bear, for I am in constant pain and cannot abide the pity or the gaze of others."

"I am truly sorry for your predicament. We were not aware of it."

"This is my punishment, my judgement for taking the wife of another man, despicable though he is. You say you know of my friendship with Elizabeth as, I dare say, do many others by now. None of it would ever have happened, had not Fyffe Hibberdson driven her away with his cruelty. His appearance does not betray it, but that man is a monster. I saw the marks of his excesses on her flesh and heard the pain in her voice, many times. The condition I am in now was brought about by a fellow who concealed his face behind a mask as he splashed me with vitriol. I have always suspected that this was Hibbertson's revenge, taken personally or by means of an agent, but I cannot prove it. Even if I could, his position in the community and my poverty would keep the case from the courts." He lowered his head, lost for a moment in recollection and regret. "But I digress, please ask what you will."

"You have already answered most of my questions by means of your most interesting narrative," said Holmes. "But there is one more issue on which I remain uncertain."

Mr Ridden leaned forward to catch my friend's enquiry, then squirmed at the painful result of his movement. "I am at your disposal."

"Please do not think that I am making light of this, when I ask: what was the colour of Mrs Hibberdson's hair?"

Astonishment crossed the disfigured face, but the answer was immediately forthcoming. "Why, Elizabeth had long tresses, of a rich brown lustre."

Holmes rose from his chair and I followed.

"That is all I wish to know. My thanks to you, sir. And I apologise again for the intrusion."

#

Holmes said nothing until we had left Cardinal Way. "We will take the long route back to the inn I think, Watson. The exercise will be beneficial as I review my findings."

"I cannot help but feel sorry for that poor fellow, Holmes. He has paid a terrible price for his indiscretion."

"And continues to do so, since he now has little choice but to live the life of a hermit."

"You are certain that Mrs Hibberdson was murdered, and did not simply flee from her husband's cruelty?"

"Quite certain. It seems certain that she and Mr Ridden had come to have considerable affection for each other. I cannot imagine her leaving the village without asking him to accompany her, or at least informing him of her destination."

Little else was said between us until we reached the inn. Because of our longer walk it was now almost time for dinner. At my friend's suggestion we each enjoyed a pint of good ale as the landlord and his wife made their preparations, and then sat down to a meal of braised steak. For once, Holmes ate with relish.

"Your appetite has improved," I observed. "A sure and certain sign that you have arrived at the solution of a case."

"I had not realized that I am so predictable, Watson," he smiled. "But you are not quite correct. There is a final piece to be fitted to the puzzle, and then my case will be complete."

"That is for tomorrow, then?"

"Not at all, old fellow. What do you say to another, but much shorter, walk after dinner? If I am right about what I expect to see, this affair will be cleared up before mid-day tomorrow, when we will be on the late morning train to London."

When our plates had been cleared away I indulged myself with a thick slice of the landlord's wife's apple pie, while Holmes looked on with some amusement as he sipped a cup of strong coffee. At the moment I finished my own coffee he got to his feet and we emerged into the street as the light faded.

Holmes was as good as his word. The work was indeed short, to the extent that we passed but a few shops and paused outside the closed establishment of Mr Fyffe Hibberdson. Holmes bent to peer at something displayed in the window and turned abruptly.

"That is sufficient. If you wish, Watson, we can now return to the inn to sit and reminisce about our past experiences together over a glass of brandy. I am quite sure that you will derive something to over-dramatize and send to your publisher."

I was surprised that our excursion was of such short duration, but the opportunity to discuss our old adventures was a rarity with Holmes. I readily agreed to his suggestion and we retraced our steps.

"You are now satisfied then, that you have solved this curious affair?"

"I am, it is now all clear to me," was all that he would say.

#

The following morning Holmes entered the inn as I sat down to breakfast, seating himself opposite me as I awaited the landlord's attention.

"There is a slight tinge of colour in your face, Holmes. Clearly, you have enjoyed a bracing walk."

"I have been to the local police station to see Inspector Carew, who seems to be a most agreeable fellow. Doubtlessly, we will see something of him later."

I was served a hearty breakfast, and Holmes again contented himself with coffee but added a single slice of toast. Already I had noticed the glitter of anticipation in his eyes, which betrayed his eagerness to savour the last act of this affair and bring it to a successful conclusion. Indeed, I had hardly consumed the last mouthful of food, before he rose abruptly.

"Come, Watson, let us complete our work here."

I stood up and hesitated. "Holmes, there is much about this that I fail to understand. Before we proceed, perhaps you could enlighten me."

"I have come to realise that there is much that I, myself, failed to comprehend at its beginning, old fellow, but all is now plain to me. As for explanations, see what you can make of this morning's activity and I will furnish a full account as we return to Baker Street."

I knew that he would say nothing more until then, so I followed him out into the morning sunshine. We walked the short distance to the office of the solicitors, Craven & Hibberdson, and paused before entering.

"You are armed, I take it?" my friend whispered.

"My service revolver is never far from me."

"Excellent."

He pushed open the door, to reveal Mr Fyffe Hibberdson speaking to a young woman, presumably his secretary, who sat before a typewriting machine.

"Mr Holmes. Doctor Watson!" His surprise was evident, and a hint of wariness crept into his face. "I had not expected to see you again. Is there something new?"

"We have made some progress," said Holmes. "But one question remains, before we return to London."

Mr Hibberdson said something to the young woman, who nodded and began to type. He gave us a suspicious glance, before ushering us into his office.

When we were all seated, he looked at us uncertainly. His weather-beaten face held a rather fixed smile.

"And so, Mr Holmes, presumably you have reached the end of your investigation. May I ask, have you achieved your objective?"

"It would be more accurate, I think, to say that events took an unexpected turn. As I said, one aspect is still unresolved."

Mr Hibberdson nodded. "It is something that you believe I am able to assist with, or you would not be here."

"It is indeed."

"Then what is it, pray?"

Holmes stood up quickly. "We wish to know where you have hidden your wife's body."

All expression left Mr Hibberdson's face, and as he rose from his chair his breathing became laboured. A stray lock of grey hair fell across his forehead.

"What do you mean," he stammered.

"Pretence is useless. We know all."

Fury crossed Mr Hibberdson's face then, and desperation. He quickly pulled out a drawer and produced a pistol, which he lowered immediately as he saw that my own was pointed at his heart. He dropped his weapon and slumped into his seat, leaning across his desk with his head in his hands.

"I was desperate," he looked up at us for understanding or sympathy, and found none. "My wife had taken up with another man, a filthy farm worker."

"She found your cruelty repugnant," I told him.

"A small measure of the whip now and then does no harm, but reminds a woman of her place. I am not an evil man, gentlemen."

Holmes fixed him with a steely stare. "Then it would be interesting to hear your explanation as to why you lay in wait for us as we returned from the Truegrace's residence. I was aware that we were followed as we left, but not that it was by yourself. The sun glinted on the barrel of your pistol, but the passing of several vehicles obscured your line of fire. Subsequently, you attempted to murder Doctor Watson and myself by sending poisoned wine to the inn."

Hibberdson hammered on his desk with his fists, completely distraught now. "Do you not see, I had to protect myself! I knew of your reputation, and it was certain that you would soon uncover what I had so carefully concealed. The risk was too great."

I let my eyes stray to a portrait above him. A stern figure, possibly the late Mr Craven, looked down.

"And it was you, of course, who disfigured Mr Ridden?"

"I could not bear to think of him escaping unscathed after affecting my life so."

"I ask you again," Holmes said harshly, where is the body of Elizabeth Hibberdson?"

Hibbersdon went very still. "She is at the bottom of Merren Lake, near the county border", he said in a quiet voice. "I could bear the humiliation she brought upon me no longer."

"Your confession solves an old mystery," said the tall sharp-faced man who had quietly entered the room. "I must now ask you to accompany me to Grovell Police Station, where you will be formally charged."

"Ah, Inspector Carew," Holmes said lightly, "arriving exactly as we arranged. I trust that what you have just witnessed, together with the full report I supplied earlier, will suffice for your purposes?"

The inspector smiled briefly, the expression appearing out of place on that harsh countenance, before replying. "It will be more than adequate, I am sure. My thanks to you and Doctor Watson for your timely assistance on this unsolved case."

My friend, looking away from Hibberdson, inclined his head in acknowledgement. "We are pleased to have been of service." He consulted his pocket-watch. "But now I see that we scarcely have time to return to Worcester for the morning train. We wish you good morning, Inspector."

#

The return journey was without mention of the case. As was sometimes his custom, Sherlock Holmes expounded on several unrelated subjects, so that my frustration had reached unbearable heights by the time we were but a few miles from London.

I turned from the window, as the train plunged into the heavy fog that had quickly settled. "Holmes, I must say that you surprised me by taking the brother and sister Truegrace seriously."

"I wondered whether you would be able to restrain your curiosity as far as Baker Street," he laughed. "I found it amusing to watch your expressions as I spoke of other things."

"Am I so obvious?"

"Not always, old fellow, and never, I would think, to the untrained eye."

"Thank you for your reassurance. Perhaps you will now furnish me with an explanation."

The train came to a halt at the last rural station before approaching the capital. On the single platform, passengers and porters moved about like grey ghosts. The fog showed no signs of lifting.

"You were surprised that I agreed to take the case, because of my aversion to the belief in the supernatural," he began. "In fact, I started with the assumption that no such thing was involved here. At first I thought, quite wrongly, that there was something sinister about the predicted demise of the maid, and that either or both of the Truegraces were somehow responsible. I was only certain of the identity of the murderer of Mrs Hibberson, when I saw the injuries inflicted on Mr Albert Ridden."

As the train began to move again, I thought about this. "I can see no connection."

"That is because you failed to notice the burns on Hibberdson's hands, when we first encountered him. They meant nothing to me at the time, but on seeing the vitriol burns on Mr Ridden, it became apparent that Hibberdson had accidentally spilled some on himself as he transferred the chemical from a large container to a portable-sized jar. At the same time, a possibility occurred to me. What if this vision of Miss Truegrace's were not of herself and her brother, but of two other people? I then asked myself who else it could have been, and recalled that we had learned of the disappearance of Hibberdson's wife after many violent clashes with her husband. I then looked for similarities between Miss Truegrace and Mrs Hibberdson – you will recall my asking Mr Ridden about the colour of Mrs Hibberdson's hair – and discovered that my theory was sound."

I could follow his reasoning, but detected a flaw.

"Holmes, are you forgetting that the woman in the vision actually named her murderer?"

"That was the final confirmation. Hence our short walk, last evening?"

I nodded. "As far as Hibberdson's office."

"Precisely. Displayed in the window was his certificate of qualification to practice in the legal profession. It bore the name 'Fyffe Jonathan Peter Cedric Hibberdson'."

Suddenly, it was all clear to me. "So Hibberdson also had the name 'Cedric', as did Mr Truegrace?"

"Indeed. I doubted our client's guilt when I saw the genuine fear in the sister's eyes, and the hurt at being thought of as a likely murderer in those of her brother. That something was amiss was a certainty, and curiosity impelled me to investigate."

"But none of this," I observed with a curious satisfaction, "explains the vision of Miss Anna Truegrace. Since it was that which led to this affair, may I take it that you now acknowledge such occurrences as reality, Holmes?"

The train slid to a gentle halt at Paddington Station and passengers, soon made indistinct by the smoke from the engine and the fog, streamed out onto the platform. My friend rose steadily, retrieving his bag and handing mine to me.

"No," he said then, "the supernatural, if it exists, remains as much a mystery as ever. But you can take it, Watson, that I am truly amazed when new capabilities of the infinitely complicated human mind reveal themselves."

The Adventure of Mr Fairdale Hobbs

During the years when I lived in Baker Street with my friend, the consulting detective Mr Sherlock Holmes, I was privileged to share many extraordinary adventures with him as he would often honour me by requesting my assistance.

There were, of course, occasional similarities between the cases, that is to say that one bank robbery was much like another. Yet I was always able, when given permission to publish an account of the circumstances at a much later date, to discern some distinguishing feature which qualified the tale as unique.

"I fear, Watson, that we must postpone further discussion of my early cases until another time. I believe I heard the door-bell just now and Mrs Hudson has admitted someone." My friend sat up straight in his chair as we prepared to fill our pipes after dinner one early summer evening.

"You have already said that you have no appointments, Holmes."

"Indeed I did, and I expected none, but this fellow whose tread on the stairs is so heavy may have brought us something interesting. Besides, I have two cases on hand that will doubtless come to fruition before the end of the month, but nothing that requires my immediate attention."

This abrupt change to the evening caused me only momentary surprise. I had long become accustomed to my friend's bohemian character, and his sudden changes of mood and intentions. We put away our pipes and waited in silence for the few moments that passed before our landlady opened the door to usher in a middle-aged man of average height, dressed in a worn but well-pressed tweed suit.

"Good evening, Mr Holmes and Doctor Watson," he said without waiting to be announced. "It is good to make your acquaintances again, sirs."

"You know us then?" I responded.

"Indeed he does, Watson," Holmes confirmed. "This is Mr Fairdale Hobbs, who you may remember from the affair immediately before that which you over-dramatized as 'The Red Circle'."

"As I recall, you said that case was hardly worth the trouble, since it was 'a simple matter'."

"Which remains an accurate description. I should have seen it all before I left this room." He glanced towards the door, having realised that our landlady was hovering. "Would you care for tea, Mr Hobbs?"

"No thank you, sir. If you don't mind, I would rather tell you what brings me here."

Holmes waited until Mrs Hudson had withdrawn, then gestured that our visitor should sit. "I think you will find the basket chair the most comfortable."

I was surprised that Holmes did not immediately recover his pipe, whereupon I would have done likewise, but it seemed that his curiosity had been aroused by the reappearance of Mr Hobbs as had my own.

"I hope you will pardon this intrusion gentlemen," Mr Hobbs said then. "I was sent to London only this afternoon, and so had not enough time to make an appointment since the nearest Post Office is further away than the railway station."

Holmes nodded. "Further away from where, pray?"

"Why, from where I live and work these days, sir. That is Gaunt Manor, in Cambridgeshire. The nearest village Willadale, is almost five miles away."

"You are no longer a lodger at Mrs Warren's house then?" I enquired.

The expected glance of annoyance at my interruption from Holmes was not forthcoming, so I concluded that he had been about to ask the same question.

"No, Doctor," Mr Hobbs replied. "That has been a good while ago now. These days I live at Gaunt Manor because I am employed there. I do just about everything to keep the place going except tend the horses. Our stable-lad, Joel, does that."

"And in whose service are you now?" Holmes asked. "The owner of Gaunt Manor, I presume."

"That's right, sir. Mrs Rosemary Prescott. I found her crying when I reported for duty this morning and, having no one else to talk to I suppose, she confessed the reason for her distress to me. We have, you see, become rather closer over the last few years than is usual between mistress and servant. Sometimes I find myself looking upon her as the daughter I never had. As soon as I grasped her problem I remembered how you once helped me and recommended you to her, but she said only that she would consider the situation. I gathered that she was reluctant to involve anyone else, for she is something of a recluse, but I was summoned just after mid-day and given leave to consult you."

"I thank you for the recommendation, Mr Hobbs," Holmes acknowledged. "Mrs Prescott is a young woman, then?"

"She is indeed, though older than she appears. She married young but was widowed less than two years ago. Mr Carlton was killed after falling off a horse. Struck by a low-hanging branch, no more than half a mile from home."

"But you already worked at Gaunt Manor while he lived?"

"For some years now, Mr Holmes." He scratched his head, thoughtfully. "The truth is, I can't remember how many. I'm getting forgetful, these days."

"This lady then, has become reclusive since her husband's death. Has she no children?"

"Oh yes, didn't I mention Alice? She must be fifteen years old, by now. Shortly after her father died, she pleaded with her mother to be allowed to join a convent. This didn't surprise Mrs Prescott a great deal, for Alice has been very religious since early childhood. Nevertheless, permission was refused at first, on account of the girl's age. Mrs Prescott was still grieving of course, but when her daughter told of her own sadness at the loss of her father she relented. I think what decided the matter was Alice's insistence that to eventually join the Sisterhood was the only way she would ever again know peace."

Holmes sat up in his chair. "Is it this young lady, who is causing such anguish to her mother?"

"Not herself, but this will explain." Mr Hobbs reached into his pocket and extracted a folded sheet of paper which he handed to my friend, who read the contents with a grim expression.

*Mrs Rosemary Prescott,*

*This is to inform you that your daughter, Alice, has been taken away from the protection of the Sisterhood of Golgotha. You can be assured that she will be cared for, and will come to no harm, until mid-day of this coming Sunday, by which time you will have paid the sum of two thousand pounds for her safe return.*

*I must impress upon you that the money must be brought to a place about which you will be advised, and by no one other than yourself. Your appearance is known to us and you will be met for the exchange. The substitution of an emissary will be viewed with the greatest suspicion and considered as a breach of faith so you must not, in any circumstances, consider such a course of action.*

*You are urged also not to attempt to consult the official police force regarding this matter. Failure to comply with this restriction will result in the loss of your chance to be reunited with your daughter, and her permanent disappearance.*

*For now, you must take no action until you hear from us.*

"It is unsigned." Holmes placed the letter upon a side-table, his brows knitted in deep thought.

"Can you make anything of it, sir?" Mr Hobbs asked eagerly.

"One or two trivial facts only. That the kidnappers, or at least one of them, are not of the lower classes is evident from the educated phrases used here. Also, the paper is of fine quality, which suggests that they are not poor. That there are more than one is obvious from the use of the words 'us' and 'we', unless this is a device employed to mislead us. The two points which immediately engage my interest are the stipulation that Mrs Prescott herself should deliver the ransom, and the importance placed upon this. Also, I am wondering about the means that these abductors could have employed, to remove the girl from the convent. By any chance, has the envelope which must have enclosed this letter, been retained?"

"I believe that Mrs Prescott, in her anguish, tore it to shreds."

"This occurs all too often and it is a pity, for the envelope invariably reveals something of the sender. But wait! I am taking it that this letter arrived by post. Is that, in fact, the case?"

Mr Hobbs shook his head. "I picked up the pieces from where Mrs Prescott had dropped them and, as far as I could tell, only her name had been written. There appeared to be other mark at all."

"So, the message was delivered by hand which tells us that the writer, or whoever brought it, is not far off. Did it not occur to you, Mr Hobbs, to immediately send a telegram to this convent in order to ascertain the circumstances of the girl's withdrawal from there?"

"I could not, sir. That place is situated in the Orkney Islands, to the north of Scotland."

"Where exactly, pray?"

"I believe it is near Skara Brae, but there is no wire service there and the order would not accept any communication in any case, for one of their strictest rules is that of isolation."

"I see." Holmes rested his chin on his steepled fingers and considered all that he had heard. After a few moments of silence had passed he rose to his feet. "Very well, Mr Hobbs, you may tell your employer that I am already at work on her case. Today is Wednesday, so we have three clear days before the kidnappers will carry out their threat. I would be obliged if you would convey these recommendations to Mrs Prescott: Firstly, she can expect the instructions for payment to include a meeting quite near to the local village or the surrounding area, and she must on no account venture forth from her home until this is arranged. If she intends to withdraw the ransom from a bank or elsewhere, she must send you with a letter of authority. I take it that she has complied with their demands, and not notified the official force?"

"It was all I could do to convince her to involve you, Mr Holmes. She was all for paying the money."

"Hopefully that will not be necessary, but perhaps it would be as well to have the sum available. Pray tell the lady that she will hear from me shortly, and request that she retain at all costs the contents of the kidnapper's next communication."

"I will convey your words to her, immediately upon my return."

"Capital. Now, if you have nothing else to tell me of this unfortunate affair, I will bid you good-day."

Mr Hobbs considered for a moment before, having thought of nothing further, becoming effusive with his thanks. I escorted him to the front door where I looked along the gas-lit street, silent at this hour. A hansom appeared suddenly and he summoned it as it passed. In an instant, he was gone.

Holmes had written a telegram, putting down his pen as I entered the room.

"To Lestrade?" I ventured.

"No, Watson. For now I think it best to keep Scotland Yard out of this. If their involvement became somehow known to the kidnappers, they might carry out their threat. I do not think so, but we cannot afford the risk."

"To whom is the telegram addressed, then?"

"To Barker, the private enquiry agent. You know that I have used him occasionally, since that affair of the Retired Colourman, as you called it. If the page-boy is still here I am afraid I must incur his displeasure, for disturbing him at this hour."

The lad answered our summons and took the message. From his expression, I concluded that Holmes had made his inconvenience worthwhile.

"You are sending Barker to Cambridge?" I asked when the boy had departed.

Holmes smiled. "I am sending Barker to the Orkney Isles. But now, dear fellow, I do believe that sleep would be advisable. After breakfast we should both pack a bag. It is you and I who will depart on an excursion to Cambridge."

#

When I presented myself for breakfast, I discovered that Holmes had written and despatched another wire.

"To Willadale," he explained, "to ensure that we have somewhere to lay our heads tonight."

"You do not think to stay at Gaunt Manor, to be on hand when anything further occurs?"

"That would be most unwise."

I nodded. "You have already made some progress, then?"

"It would be more accurate to say that I have come to understand that things are not the way they appear, in this affair. But come, Watson, let us waste no time in consuming our breakfasts, for my Bradshaw tells me that our train to Cambridge leaves in little more than an hour. I believe I hear Mrs Hudson on the stairs already."

And so we ate more quickly than usual, refraining from calling for a second pot of coffee. We spoke little, but as we rose from the table Holmes turned to me.

"Your bag is packed, I take it?"

"Since before I retired, last night."

"And your revolver?"

"With me, as always."

He reached for his hat and coat. "Excellent. Stout fellow."

The hurried journey through the East End of London to Bishopsgate Station was passed mostly in silence. The hansom left us before we boarded the train with minutes to spare, and my only memory until we reached our destination is of our conversation that referred to a previous case of abduction – that which I have recorded as 'The Adventure of the Priory School', concerning the young Lord Saltire and his father, the Duke of Holdernesse.

"No, Watson," my friend assured me, "I do not expect this business to turn out in the same fashion. Some of the features are quite different."

"You believe that this unfortunate girl will be murdered by her kidnappers?"

"I have every reason to doubt that. However, it is by no means impossible unless I have made a grave error of judgement. There is little point in theorizing at this stage, we must be patient while events play themselves out before us."

Beyond that, he would say nothing of his expectations. We arrived at Cambridge in the late afternoon, and Holmes consulted the local time-table, announcing that we had only fifteen minutes to wait. The train that took us down the branch line was a small and uncomfortable conveyance, but we soon found ourselves carrying our bags along the platform of the tiny Willadale Station.

The elderly man who waited with his cart near the station exit struck me as a very honest fellow.

"Of course I know the Crossed Swords, sir. I've lived here all my life and I can tell you that the rooms are clean and the food plentiful and good. It's not worth me taking you though, you just walk to the end of the lane before you turn left. You can't miss it then."

"My thanks to you," Holmes replied. "You would, I think, know everyone hereabouts, since you have always lived locally?"

"That be true, sir. There can't be many that I'm not acquainted with."

"Perhaps then, you can tell me where I am likely to find a young fellow who once worked for a friend of mine. His name is Joel, a stable lad, although I must confess to forgetting his other name."

The old fellow took off his cap and scratched his grey head. "Ah," he remembered after a moment, "You must mean Joel Crabber. Well, he's still a stable lad, or so I hear, at a place called Gaunt Manor, some distance along the road that meets this one at the crossroads back there. Thinking about it, I'd say you're in luck, because Joel comes to the village every Friday morning to buy horse feed. If you were to wait near the corn merchants shop, just down the road from the Crossed Swords and opposite the police station, you're bound to run into him at about ten o'clock."

Holmes thanked the man again, and gave him a half-sovereign for his trouble. The inn proved to be as the fellow had described and, after unpacking our few things in our rooms, we spent an hour smoking together in a comfortable lounge.

"Why are you interested in the stable lad?" I enquired when we had settled ourselves. "According to Mr Hobbs, he plays no part in this business."

My friend blew out a cloud of pungent smoke. "He hardly mentioned him, Watson, it is true. But if you recall the letter from the kidnappers, it displays certain familiarities. The title of the religious order, for instance, and the daughter's name, is known to them."

"You mean that they were informed by someone working at, or in some way close to, Gaunt Manor?"

"Indeed. They had to have a local agent, who may or may not be concerned with the abduction. You will recall that Mr Hobbs remarked that Joel was the only servant, besides himself."

"He also stated that Mrs Prescott is something of a recluse, remaining in her home since her husband's death. Why, then, would the kidnappers insist that she should deliver the ransom personally?"

"I believe I may be able to throw some light upon that, shortly. I have told the landlord that I expect a telegram either this evening or tomorrow. Unless he has changed his methods considerably, Barker will have obtained the information that I requested by then. But look, old fellow, some of the other guests are already making their way to the dining-room. I suggest that we do likewise and continue our conversation over dinner."

But there was no word from Barker at dinner, nor at breakfast the following morning. It was not yet ten o'clock when Holmes and I took up a position near the police station, a place where we appeared to be discussing the sartorial examples in the tailor's shop window while, in reality, we closely observed the arriving customers at the corn merchants.

Three carts presented themselves, all containing a driver and passenger. Then a trap with a single occupant came to a halt near the entrance.

Holmes shook his head. "Too old. Joel has been described or confirmed as a young fellow, by both Mr Hobbs and our friend at the station."

I looked up and down the street, where an occasional hansom and four-wheeler made an appearance, but saw nothing of interest.

"It is now twenty minutes past the hour," I saw from my pocket-watch. "Perhaps he will come on a different day."

"No, Watson," Holmes pointed to the end of the street, where a cart was driven at speed past the inn. "Unless I am much mistaken, here is our stable lad. He is late today, I think."

We waited until the boy had hurriedly entered the shop and emerged, about ten minutes later, with another fellow helping to load several heavy sacks onto his cart. When that was finished the helper disappeared back into the shop and the lad took up the reins. As we walked past, Holmes held the horse's head.

The lad was about to voice his objections, but Holmes was quicker.

"Not yet, Master Crabber," he said. "I wish to speak to you."

The boy's glare was hostile. "I don't know you! Who are you?"

"My name is Sherlock Holmes. I am a consulting detective from London. It has come to my notice that you are involved in a conspiracy to extort money from your employer."

The boy took on a furtive look at once, and I knew that Holmes' identification was correct. "Who says so, then?"

"The evidence is quite clear. I confess to being at a loss to imagine how you thought you would remain unpunished, now that your accomplice has confessed. You were instrumental in putting Mrs Prescott's daughter in mortal danger. It is well known that kidnappers invariably murder their victims, so as to prevent them from identifying them to the police. At the very least, you will be charged as an accessory."

"But he swore Alice would come to no harm, if I told him where she is living!" Crabber's face was now full of alarm. "I swear, Mr Holmes, I never knew there would be murder. Oh, my God," he put his hands to is face and wept, all defiance gone. "What can I do?"

"If you are truthful with me, I will do what I can for you," Holmes said in an even tone. "We believe that your co-conspirator has given us a false name. If you tell us who he truly is, and where he has been hiding, it will go well with you."

"He is Mr Grenville Prescott!" the lad wailed.

"A relation of your employer?"

"Her brother-in-law. The younger brother of her deceased husband."

"I presume he paid you for your services?"

Crabber averted his eyes. "He gave me five pounds."

"He pays well, indeed. Where is he now?"

"I had to visit him, to tell him about Alice. He rents a cottage in Little Bursford. The address is 2, Pear Tree Grove."

My friend nodded. "How far is that, from here?"

"You turn left at the end of this street." The lad pointed past the library, to where we could see the entrance to a wide lane. "If you go straight for a mile and a half, you will be there."

"I am obliged to you for your frankness," Holmes said. "You must tell no one of our conversation and, as I have already promised, I will convey a favourable impression of you because you did not fully realise the likely consequences of your actions."

"Thank you, sir."

"But you must swear to never again be tempted by the lure of easy profit. Such arrangements are almost always rooted in dishonesty."

Crabber lowered his head, ashamed of his small part in this. "Yes, I swear."

"Then we will bid you good-day."

#

"You certainly put fear into that ruffian, Holmes," I remarked when we had walked well out of earshot.

"A little too much, perhaps. I deplore his betrayal of his employer, but I cannot believe that he is the criminal type."

"Is that why you promised to speak for him?"

He shrugged his shoulders. "His only crime, after all, was to tell this man Grenville Prescott where his niece is living. As much could have transpired during normal conversation. Nevertheless, we have done some good here. Crabber will not easily stray down the wrong road, I think."

"Were you surprised to learn that the kidnapper is the late Mr Prescott's brother?"

"Not entirely. One of the suppositions that I had formed about this case was that a relation of some sort might be involved. You see, Watson, if Mrs Prescott is a recluse, seeing no one, then it is likely that her tormenter is someone close. Who else does a friendless woman have, but her family?"

He said little else then, as we walked around that charming village until the hour for luncheon arrived. My thoughts were occupied with theories of my own, and wondering if we were to enlist the aid of the local force to arrest this man Grenville Prescott. I also reflected that Holmes' leniency with the stable boy had revealed a glimpse of the compassionate heart that beats within the breast of the man who was known, to almost all that he had ever encountered, as the calculating reasoner whose emotions could be likened to the workings of a machine.

"I presume we will be visiting Little Bursford, this afternoon?" I ventured as we concluded our luncheon with cups of strong coffee.

"Your presumption is correct. I must ask the landlord if he knows anyone from whom we can hire a trap for a couple of hours. Our business should take no longer than that."

At just that moment the fellow appeared. He was a portly man of about fifty, red-faced and smiling.

"The telegram you were expecting, Mr Holmes."

My friend took it from the tray. "My thanks to you, landlord. I wonder, are you aware of anyone who could let us have a trap for an hour or two?"

"I can think of several, sir, but none of them are nearby. You might be better, if you don't mind using such a conveyance, to borrow the cart that we use for deliveries of one kind or another.

You'll find the horse grazing in the field at the back of the inn, and the cart is kept in the yard."

"Many thanks, once again," Holmes said as the man took our used cups and departed. He tore open the envelope eagerly.

"Did the wire reveal anything?" I asked before he could rise.

He nodded. "Barker has found exactly what I had begun to suspect."

He paused as the noise from the surrounding tables increased. A man who looked like a local farmer had amused his companions by drinking a pint of ale with singular speed.

I looked at Holmes expectantly but he said nothing more, instead sliding the telegram towards me.

It contained a single sentence: *All is well with the Sisterhood of Golgotha.*

"What does this mean?" I asked in astonishment.

"Simply that there has been no kidnapping, after all. There is something deeper here, I think."

We accepted the landlord's offer and were soon on our way in his cart, pulled by a lively young colt who accepted the control of the reins reluctantly. Crabber had not misinformed us, for the distance to Little Bursford was indeed no more than a mile and a half. We emerged from a wide and leafy lane, with fields on either side, to be confronted with a village of small thatched cottages with an ancient church at the distant end of the central street. We had no difficulty in finding Pear Tree Grove, since the sign near the village green had been newly painted. Number two was identical to several other dwellings, except the door-knocker was shaped like a tiger's head and had been polished to a fine gloss.

Holmes rapped on the door but once with his stick, as I tethered the horse to the fence at the edge of the field that faced the house. The door opened at once, to reveal a tall thin man of ghostly white pallor.

"Come in, gentlemen," he said at once. "I have been expecting you."

We entered and were bidden to sit. The man held up a half-empty whisky bottle, but we both declined.

"How is it that you knew we would come, Mr Prescott," I enquired.

He let his gaze roam around the room, taking in the brass warming pans and oak beams as if searching for words. "We have heard of the exploits of Mr Holmes even here, and of your recording of them, Doctor. As for your presence in my temporary home, I knew because word travels very quickly about new arrivals in the villages. From the moment I heard your name, I knew my game was up."

"Did you really intend to kill your sister-in-law?" Holmes asked.

I gave him a surprised glance, for I had not expected a mention of murder.

"Perhaps I would have done, had my plan succeeded and she had delivered the ransom, believing that her daughter had been abducted. Since my brother's death she has hardly ventured from Gaunt Manor, but I knew this would entice her. However," Mr Prescott held up a quivering hand, "the burden of guilt that I would assume has already had its effect upon me. I cannot sleep, and my meals have been replaced by whisky."

"Clearly, you are no murderer, but how did this situation arise? If there is a dispute of some sort between you, could you not have visited her and come to some arrangement?"

Our host shook his head in despair. " I will acquaint you with the full facts, and then you will understand."

He turned to a writing-desk in the corner of the room. From a drawer he took a single sheet of paper and handed it to Holmes. My friend cast his eyes over it quickly.

"Your brother is the author of this?" he enquired.

"He sent it to me in London, shortly before his death. That is why I came to live here."

"To wreak vengeance?"

"How else could I act, in the circumstances?"

"Is there proof of this, elsewhere perhaps?"

Mr Prescott lowered himself into a chair, his head bowed. "In Willadale there is the firm of solicitors, Warren, Candale & Monk. They represented my brother for many years, and he wrote an identical account in their office in front of witnesses. As for the document you hold in your hand, you may retain it if you wish."

Holmes nodded his head. "Very well, Mr Prescott, I will take this document, and we will certainly pay this concern a visit. As for you, if you have spoken truthfully you have committed no crime except to make threats by means of the letter you delivered to your sister-in-law, and when truth prevails your actions will attract no punishment. I recommend that you return to London to resume your life there, with the assurance that justice will be done without any risk to your freedom."

We left him then, unmistakeably grieving but somehow, I felt, surrounded by an air of relief.

#

Holmes said little as we drove back to Willadale. He appeared deep in thought, but I was confused by this latest development. Finally, before our journey was even half over, I could contain myself no longer.

"I had thought, Holmes, that Mr Prescott would be arrested for the attempted kidnapping of his niece. What has transpired, to absolve him?"

"All will become clear to you, Watson, when we visit Gaunt Manor tomorrow morning. We will go directly there after consulting Warren, Candale & Monk, in Willadale."

He would say nothing more, avoiding all my subsequent attempts to procure enlightenment in favour of an extensive lecture about the connection of Oliver Cromwell to the Cambridge area. This he insisted upon continuing throughout dinner, and I confess to being somewhat relieved when we retired to the lounge with our pipes. During the evening we consumed two glasses of a fine old brandy that the landlord recommended and Holmes, at last changing the subject of his discourse, revealed to me the details of a case which took place before our association. At some future time I hope for this to be published, with his permission, probably under the title 'The Adventure of the Broken Chalice'.

Next morning, his eagerness for breakfast to be over was obvious.

"Come, Watson, finish your toast and coffee and we will proceed. I have already ascertained from the landlord that the offices of Warren, Candale & Monk are situated near the undertaker's premises in Catherine Street."

131

We presented ourselves as a young clerk opened the doors to begin the business of the day. In answer to our enquiries he informed us that Mr Monk had recently passed away and Mr Warren was away at present. He would seek however, an audience with Mr Candale, provided that no appointments for this time had already been arranged.

We were summoned, after about ten minutes, to a rather soberly furnished office that smelled strongly of wood polish. Mr Candale was a tall, thin gentleman who was well into his old age. His body was angular, his movements stiff and his dress funereal.

"Good morning, gentlemen," he gave a slight bow and bade us be seated, before settling himself behind the massive desk that took up much of the room. "Pray tell me how I can assist you."

My friend introduced us, explaining that we were in the village in the course of an enquiry. "I have been given a document, sir, and it is imperative that I confirm it as genuine."

"What does the document contain?"

"It is an account of events that occurred shortly before the death of one of your clients, Mr Carlton Prescott, written in his own hand. It is his brother, Mr Grenville Prescott, who has sent us to you because a similar account was written here in front of witnesses."

Mr Candale rubbed his chin. "I remember the occasion well, for I, myself, was among the witnesses. The signatures were only to confirm that it was the hand of Mr Carlton Prescott that wrote the account. What the contents were I do not know, and neither do the others who signed, since the document was immediately sealed and consigned to our safe at the writer's request, where it has remained ever since."

"I would be obliged," said Holmes, "if you would retrieve it for comparison with the account that I have here. It is crucial that I ascertain that the author is the same."

"I can vouch for the version that we have retained, of course."

"As for the other, I have the word of Mr Grenville Prescott."

Mr Candale's expression became more serious. "If you will furnish me with written authority from him, I will produce that which was left with us."

"Mr Prescott has given us no such thing, but I will request that he attends personally within the next few days, for the purposes of confirmation."

"I am sorry, gentlemen," the solicitor got to his feet awkwardly, "but I cannot accede to such a request without some form of authority. If you can obtain this I will be glad to oblige, but for now I will wish you both good day."

Holmes stood and I saw the steely glint of determination in his eyes. "Sir, I should tell you that to delay might well permit a murderer to escape justice. It would be a more speedy solution to wire Scotland Yard, with a view to obtaining reassurance as to my discretion."

Then began a long contemplative silence, during which Mr Candale became even more solemn.

"Very well," he said at last. "In view of the fact that you are a consulting detective – oh yes, I have heard of your work assisting Scotland Yard, Mr Holmes – and the circumstances that you describe, I will retrieve the document that was left in our care. After all, as you have said, all that you require is to ascertain that the two accounts were written by the same hand."

"Precisely." Holmes confirmed with a scowl on his face. Any reference to him as an assistant to the official force, to which he had so many times presented a completed case in advance of their own investigations, was certain to produce this effect. "I am obliged to you, Mr Candale."

#

Later that morning we found ourselves, having again prevailed upon the landlord for the hire of his cart, handing the conveyance over to a very subdued Joel in the courtyard of Gaunt Manor.

I must confess that the first thought to enter my head as the place came into sight was that it fully deserved its title. It was a structure of grey stone, covered in moss in many places, comprising of a short central corridor or gallery which led from either end to decaying wings with tall windows.

"Hardly an attractive place, Holmes", I remarked as we walked across uneven flagstones with weeds sprouting between them.

"Late Tudor or early Stuart, I would think. That design was quite common during those periods. But look, that rather warped door is opening and I see Mr Fairdale Hobbs is waiting to greet us. He is innocent, but I do not think he will come well out of this. I fear we may have to forego luncheon, Watson, for I do not expect our business here to be over quickly."

Our client could hardly contain himself. As we reached the top of the steps he emerged and confronted us expectantly.

"Have you made progress, Mr Holmes?" he asked as soon as he had greeted us.

"I have. All is now clear to me."

Relief swept over Mr Hobbs' face. "Then Alice will be returned?"

"Alice was never absent, nor was she at any time in danger."

"I am afraid I do not understand."

"If Mrs Prescott permits you to remain as we interview her, you will quickly comprehend the true nature of the situation. You presented these circumstances to us as a tragedy, and I will tell you that the truth of them is indeed a tragedy. If you would conduct us into your employer's presence, I would be obliged."

Mr Hobbs could have had no conception as to what Holmes was about to reveal, but he sensed that the news would not be pleasant. As he led us into  a long corridor, I saw that his countenance had become visibly grey.

We were shown into a room with much overstuffed furniture. A woman lay draped across a chaise-longue near the tall open windows with her back to us. She rose and turned to face us as we approached.

"Mr Sherlock Holmes and Doctor Watson," Mr Hobbs announced.

She smiled and nodded. "The gentlemen we engaged to rescue my daughter, of course. I take it that you have succeeded?"

Mrs Prescott  possessed considerable beauty, although well past the first flush of her youth. In a costume of dark green, her shoulder-length hair shone in the light from the windows, and I saw that she had preserved her figure well. It was not until the wariness of her expression and the wildness of her eyes were noticed, that she could have been perceived as a woman somewhat deranged.

"On that score, madam, you need have no fear. Your daughter was never kidnapped, nor was she in any sort of danger."

"But," she began, aghast, "the letter, the threats?"

"All with a single purpose – to cause you to leave this house."

"For what reason? I do not understand this."

"It was a device to provide an opportunity for your murder."

All colour left her face, and Mr Hobbs, who had remained without seeking her permission, drew nearer to her.

"Who would contemplate such a thing?" she asked in a whisper.

"I am sure that you already know the answer to that, unless you have other enemies. It is your brother-in-law, Mr Grenville Prescott."

"Grenville? I have not seen him since my husband's death."

"That is hardly surprising. Having killed his brother it would be truly strange if he had friendly intentions toward you."

"What can you mean by that?" But her face had changed to that of a furtive animal. She was ready to defend herself, but knew the battle was already lost.

"There was no riding accident. You struck your husband with some sort of bludgeon, probably a fallen branch, and successfully maintained the deceit."

She collected herself quickly, her voice harsher now. "Why would I do such a thing? Carlton and I were close and had much affection for each other. I loved him!"

"I believe that you did," Holmes affirmed, "and sadly, that was why you took his life. You had for some time suspected him of conducting regular assignations with a woman living in Little Bursford, and I suspect that the strain of this growing resentment became too much for you. When you could tolerate it no longer, you murdered him."

"Carlton was secretive about some things," she said, and at that moment tears began to flow, signalling her capitulation. "He would not talk of it, and I could not bear to share him."

"Neither did you," Holmes said in a voice that was almost kindly. "It is true that he visited a woman, but it was the sister of a fallen army comrade who is blind. He helped her, as he had sworn to do, with food and a nurse to ensure her welfare."

"That is why you described these events as a true tragedy," Mr Hobbs realised then.

"Indeed. Your husband was disturbed by your worsening behaviour," my friend continued to Mrs Prescott, "and came to realise that you had become irrational. It is clear from his writings that he expected some sort of attack, but probably not a murderous one."

The room was silent for several moments, the only sounds were the cries of the captive peacocks that I could see caged among the colourful flowers of the garden.

"So this was to be Grenville's revenge!" Mrs Prescott burst out suddenly. "But how could he have known of how things lay between Carlton and myself? How did you discover all this, Mr Holmes?"

Holmes took the letter from his pocket. "As I have stated, your husband sensed impending conflict between you. He wrote a full account of his fears, which he left with his brother. Another

137

copy was left with his solicitor. I have compared them, and there is no question but that they were written by the same hand."

"If only your husband and yourself had talked about the situation, this would never have come about," I remarked to her. "He would have been alive to this day."

"All men and women have their secrets," Holmes acknowledged. "Sometimes for the most extraordinary and unnecessary reasons. Mr Hobbs, may I prevail upon you to ride to Willadale and inform the constable there of what you have witnessed this morning?" Watson and I will remain with Mrs Prescott, until you return."

During his absence she sat staring into the far distance, tearful but not speaking. I considered that Mrs Prescott was more likely to end her days in an asylum than at the end of a hangman's rope, and I could not help but pity her. Very little conversation between Holmes and myself ensued, until Mr Hobbs returned in the company of Constable Hutchins, who led his prisoner away after acquainting himself with the circumstances.

"The daughter will doubtless be cared for by the Sisters of Golgotha," Holmes said as we were about to leave. He turned then to regard Mr Fairdale Hobbs, who stood, an uncertain and dejected figure, near the door. "I see, Mr Hobbs, that you are saddened by your altered circumstances. You are now without employment, indeed without a roof over your head since Gaunt Manor will certainly be sold and the proceeds invested for the benefit of Alice Prescott. It may have crossed your mind that none of this would have arisen, had you not consulted me at Baker Street. Nevertheless, you have the satisfaction of knowing that you were instrumental in causing justice to be done where the need was not previously perceived. I tell you not to concern yourself about your situation or your lodgings. In the course of my work I have acquired many who I can call upon for assistance and support, and

I would not be at all surprised to hear that your difficulties are settled before this week is out."

# The Adventure of the Conk-Singleton Forgery

Once more searching among my notes recording the extraordinary adventures of my friend Mr Sherlock Holmes at the request of my publisher, I have discovered a case so far untold to the general public. On approaching my friend, I was given grudging permission to relate it to the best of my recollection.

He had, in fact, given the matter some thought before the affair I later entitled 'The Adventure of the Six Napoleons' was brought to our attention by Inspector Lestrade and, when that was settled, Holmes lost no time in resorting to a study of the letter which we had previously received.

"The writer was rather vague, Watson. I have learned from Burke's Peerage that Mr Edward Conk-Singleton is the only son of Lord Andersley and deduced from his mention of forgery that he has been defrauded in some way, but that is all." He paused for an instant, and then added, "Apart, that is, from my surprise at his use of such poor quality writing paper and envelope, which suggests that he is no longer as prosperous as formerly."

I placed my empty coffee cup to one side, with my used plate. "Have you now replied to him?"

"I did so when Lestrade presented us with the affair that we concluded yesterday, informing Mr Conk-Singleton that I would give his problem my attention at the first opportunity. Now that I am able to do this I have contacted him by telegraph. There has been no reply, so I presume he has agreed with my suggestion that he should visit us in about," he took out his pocket-watch and glanced at it. "ten minutes from now."

Holmes immediately called for Mrs Hudson, who appeared promptly to take away the remains of our breakfasts. I sought out my notebook and ensured that my pencil was sharp, wondering whether our visitor would conform to the aristocratic image that I had formed in my mind.

We had settled in our chairs and almost finished our first cigarettes of the day, when the door-bell rang and our landlady answered. Holmes and I exchanged puzzled glances as we overheard her tone, which was remarkably similar to that reserved for Wiggins and the Baker Street Irregulars.

"He is five minutes late," my friend observed.

For a moment there was silence, save for the rattle of a four-wheeler outside. Then I heard a heavy tread upon the stairs. Holmes and I turned towards the door as it opened to admit our client, who was immediately announced in disapproving tones by Mrs Hudson.

Holmes stared at the man in silence for an instant, as our landlady retreated.

"Mr Conk-Singleton," he said, rising. "Do come in and make yourself comfortable. I am Sherlock Holmes, and this is Doctor John Watson whose assistance I have found to be invaluable and in whom you may confide as you would in me."

After we had shaken hands, I studied the fellow as he seated himself. He was of average height and the exact opposite of the sort of man I had expected. His hair and beard were over-long, not tended for some time and, together with his worn pea-coat, this gave him a Bohemian look.

"Before we begin," my friend said, "allow me to call for some tea, or coffee if you prefer."

141

Our visitor held up a hand. "No, not for me, thank you, Mr Holmes. I am anxious to lay the facts of my case before you and return to my work."

"That would be the portrait or landscape you are in the midst of creating. Very well then, let us proceed."

Mr Conk-Singleton regarded Holmes with an astonished stare. "How could you know that? What do you know of me?"

"Only what my works of reference tell me, that you are the son of Lord Andersley."

"I would rather be known for my art, than for my heritage. How did you conclude that I am an artist? Has my father been here?"

This was evidently a matter of concern to him, for red patches had appeared on both his cheeks.

Holmes smiled faintly, and kept his voice to an even tone.

"I have never had the pleasure of making your father's acquaintance. As for my identification of your profession, when I see that your fingernails and indeed, your boots, are stained with paint of various colours and that you have – forgive me – adopted the appearance of one who lives an unorthodox existence, what else am I to deduce?"

"Oh yes, I see. It was quite simple, really."

Holmes scowled, as I had known him do before when, as he saw it, his skills had been belittled.

"A further observation would be, perhaps, that your father has likely disinherited you, and there is no mystery about that also. The effect that the mention of his name produced told me of your anger or disapproval of him, and your apparel would undoubtedly be of finer quality had he been kindly disposed to your chosen way of living."

A parade of expressions crossed our client's face, and for some moments I expected him to explode into a rage. As it was he became suddenly much calmer, and when he next spoke it was in a quite normal manner.

"I see that your reputation is well earned, Mr Holmes."

"Perhaps you could describe to us the nature of your difficulty," I said, with my notebook ready, to break the short silence that had ensued.

"Your letter mentioned  forgery, I think," Holmes reminded him.

Our client nodded. "I have been puzzled by it, these five weeks past, since the day I wrote to you. It is a strange situation, and I can see no purpose or reason in it."

"Pray begin at the beginning," Holmes leaned forward in his chair, "omitting not the smallest detail."

"It has been almost a year now, since I was obliged to leave my father's house," Mr Conk-Singleton reflected. "I stayed for short periods with various friends, and eventually secured accommodation in Stepney and found myself an attic studio in nearby Bethnal Green. For some months I was able to support myself by painting miniature portraits, usually of the children of clients met  through acquaintances or in taverns frequented by local artists, actors and the like. All was proceeding well, although I had to miss a meal or two, until the day I was approached by a woman called Marie Dubois."

"She visited you at your studio?" asked Holmes.

"She did. One afternoon I turned from my easel to find her standing there. I was quite surprised as I am used to complete privacy as I work, but she closed the door after her and said at once that she wished to commission me to paint her portrait."

"Did she indicate that she had been recommended?"

Our client shook his head. "Now that you mention it, Mr Holmes, I recall that she avoided answering when I asked how she knew of me. I suppose I had become excited at the prospect that I was becoming well-known."

"Undoubtedly. Did you then begin this venture?"

"I agreed immediately. She came to me three times weekly until the painting attained its present state, which is near completion."

"You will have no difficulty then, in describing her?"

"None whatsoever. She is of above average height, I would say, with a rather dark complexion and very black hair. She has a French way of speaking our language of course, but I quickly became used to it although I do not speak that tongue and we were able to converse quite easily. I learned that she is originally from Marseilles, but now lives in Paris and is in England to visit a number of friends."

"What subsequently occurred, to cause you to be discontented with this situation?"

"It was about seven weeks ago that I finished her image on the canvas, and begun on the background," he said after taking a moment for recollection. "She had described to me a scene of surrounding trees and a forest fence, and seemed pleased with my interpretation of her wishes. I should mention here perhaps that when I first occupied the studio it was in a filthy condition, and I was obliged to clean it thoroughly. Also, if I say it myself, I am meticulous in clearing up at the end of each day, so it was strange indeed that I should arrive one morning to find paint drops spilled upon the floorboards and one of my easels moved out of place. At first I thought it was my own absent-mindedness, but when this occurred subsequently I knew that someone was gaining entry overnight."

Holmes interest deepened suddenly. I recognised the glitter in his eyes from of old.

"Did these signs appear randomly, or immediately after painting a particular person?"

"That is what I was about to say, Mr Holmes, the indications were present only after the visits of Miss Dubois."

"Did you mention them to her?"

"No, I did not see how she could be concerned."

"Doubtlessly you remained in your studio overnight subsequently, to get to the truth of the matter."

"Of course, I began to do this. With the lights extinguished I forced myself to stay awake until dawn following the day of her next departure, but to no avail."

"Did you inform the lady of your intention to keep watch?"

"Not that I recall, but it is possible that I may have mentioned it."

Holmes considered for a moment. "Did her behaviour change, subsequently?"

"It did, for it was then that she began to miss appointments. When next I saw her I asked, in an indirect manner, why her attendances had become irregular, rather than according to the thrice weekly arrangement we had formerly, and she replied that this was because only the background scene of the portrait was still unfinished and that did not require her presence. She now called in, she said, only to view the progress of the painting, so that she could anticipate its delivery."

"Have these night visits continued since then?" I asked, when I saw that Holmes had paused for reflection.

"They have, Doctor, but now I have no way of knowing when to expect them."

"And you have found no alteration to your work?"

"None."

Holmes abandoned his brief reverie. "Mr Conk-Singleton, have you, yourself, formed any theory which could explain these happenings?"

Our client nodded vigorously. "The misplaced easel and the spots of paint can mean only one thing. Someone is gaining entry to my studio and copying my work! I cannot speculate as to why because, God knows, I am far from famous, but this unfinished portrait is being forged progressively. I would like you gentlemen to keep a closer watch on my studio, nightly if possible, since there are two of you, and apprehend the culprit. Until now I have not approached the official force because I felt that my case would be taken lightly, but if we were able to present the forger to them they could hardly fail to proceed."

"Quite so," Holmes confirmed. "Your studio is in Bethnel Green, I believe you said?"

"It is, at 37 Kirkfield Road."

"How would you describe it?"

"It is one long room only, with a window overlooking the street and a large skylight at the opposite end. There is one room below, which was occupied by the late owner, and both premises are accessible only by a single staircase."

"Excellent. And, of course, you were able to see no indications of forced entry following the night visits?"

"That puzzled me also, but there were none."

"Have there been any other unusual occurrences, either in your building or nearby, since you were approached with the commission to portray Miss Dubois on canvas?"

"Only the suicide of the owner who lived below, Mr Abel Leech. But this could have no connection, surely."

Holmes straightened himself in his chair, his face impassive. "That has yet to be established, I think. As far as you know, was the official force satisfied that Mr Leech's death was by his own hand?"

"I was interviewed, because of the close proximity of my studio to the dead man's rooms, by Inspector Gregson of Scotland Yard. He seemed certain that the circumstances were as they appeared."

"How did Mr Leech bring about his own demise?"

"I was told that he hung himself, in his sitting room."

"Well," said Holmes as he rose from his chair, "you have certainly brought a curious situation to our attention, Mr Conk-Singleton. Tell me, are you returning to your studio now?"

147

"Not for several hours. I have to visit a friend concerning another matter."

"You would have no objection then, to our visiting Mr Leech's rooms in your absence?"

Our client looked totally surprised. "Of course not, but I cannot see how that will advance your investigation. Also, I am unsure as to how to obtain the key."

"Pray have no concern on those scores, but I think it would be as well if you prolonged the completion of your work for the moment. I think that I can promise you that you will hear from us before very long. And now, sir, I will bid you good day. Doctor Watson will show you out."

As often happens, our client appeared bewildered at this rather sudden dismissal, but I was able to reassure him concerning Holmes' methods as we descended the stairs.

"A somewhat peculiar fellow," Holmes said as I returned to our sitting-room.

"I knew it, the instant I saw him."

"And what, pray, did you base your assessment upon?"

I glanced at him with surprise. "Really, Holmes, you of all people. Is it not obvious from his apparel? Brown boots, in town? That is unconventional enough I would have thought, but combined with dark grey trousers?"

A smile crept across my friend's face. "As I have long maintained, we will make a detective out of you yet, Watson."

#

We arrived in Kirkfield Road shortly before mid-day. The hansom left us a short distance away at Holmes' request, and I realised that he wished our visit to pass unobserved as far as possible.

The building where Mr Conk-Singleton employed his creative talents was not impressive. Like most of those adjacent to it, maintenance had been sadly neglected. As we approached, we saw that a money-lender plied his trade from next door, while a rather shabby pie-shop operated from the opposite side. Holmes pushed open a long-unpainted door and we stepped in to be confronted by a gloomy staircase. There were but two doors, one on our immediate left and one at the top of the stairs. Clearly, these premises had once been part of a much larger house, perhaps been connected to those now occupied by the money-lender.

The stairs were dusty and the walls peeling with the remains of dull olive-green paint. The aroma from the pie-shop was not appealing. Holmes wrinkled his nose with distaste and produced his pick-lock, which quickly gained us entrance to Mr Leech's rooms .

"Stay near the door for a moment, Watson. I see that Gregson and company and any number of others have probably ruined any chance there might have been of learning anything, but it is as well to be certain. The carpet has been repositioned and the furniture put in order against the wall." He took a measuring tape from his pocket and ascertained the height of one of the three identical chairs. "The table is of sufficient weight to require several men to move it. Mr Leech must, therefore, have stood upon a chair with the noose around his neck. Although the rope has been removed, the place of its attachment to the ceiling is obvious, since the heavy gas chandelier was taken down and, as you see, stored over there in the corner. The additional accommodation appears to consist of a tiny kitchen and a single bedroom, where I expect to find the final clue to confirm my theory. We will expand our search, I think."

The kitchen yielded nothing of interest. We entered the rather drab bedroom then, and Holmes looked around carefully before opening the wardrobe. He withdrew a threadbare suit and spread it upon the bed, measuring it while I watched.

"There is nothing more to be gained from remaining here. I now know what took place."

"What occurred here, Holmes?"

"Mr Abel Leech was murdered."

"Are you certain?" I asked, feeling foolish the moment the words left my mouth.

"Quite certain."

He said no more until we had left the rooms and re-locked the door. "Now, let us see what the studio will reveal to us."

We ascended the dull staircase and entered Mr Conk-Singleton's studio, gaining admittance in the same manner. It was indeed as he had described it, with a window overlooking the street and a skylight situated at the opposite end of a long room. It did not surprise me that the fellow was untidy in his habits, with brushes and blank canvases scattered indiscriminately, or that his cleaning of the place fell far short of his claim. Holmes spent a moment in absolute stillness, his eyes taking in every detail of the chamber. They came to rest on an easel bearing the portrait of a strikingly handsome woman, presumably she who had commissioned it.

"There, Watson, the paint splashes on the floor near the easel, do you see? Notice that the colours are as used on the portrait plus one that is different." He gazed at the painting for a little while before turning his attention to the bare floorboards near the door. "Here we have part of a footprint in the fine layer of dust. If our client wears the same boots when working here as he did in Baker Street, then there has indeed been an intruder, since this impression is of a quite different style." At that he proceeded to walk all around the room, but if he saw anything more of significance he did not share it.

"Very well," he said at last. "We will now return to Baker Street to discover what Mrs Hudson has in store for us. When luncheon is over, I think a visit to Scotland Yard will be in order."

I enjoyed my roast lamb with mint sauce immensely, but Holmes ate with indifference. This came as no surprise to me, as I knew that he thought of little else when occupied with a case. The instant that I pushed my empty dessert plate away, he leapt to his feet.

"If you have no objection, Watson, I think we will forego coffee. I am anxious to find Gregson at his office, so the sooner we get to the Yard the better it will be."

"As you say, Holmes." I rose from my seat and took up my hat and coat. He did likewise and in minutes we stood in Baker Street, his stick raised to summon a passing hansom.

On the way I tried several times to extract from him an explanation as to whatever he had concluded at 37 Kirkfield Road, but he would not be drawn.

"A little patience, old fellow, and you and Gregson shall know all that I have discovered," was his only utterance, before he began to silently observe the passing scene. We were fortunate to find that Inspector Gregson had returned only hours before, from a burglary case in Mayfair.

The Scotland Yard man shook his flaxen head. "As I recall, Mr Holmes, my investigation revealed that this Mr Abel Leech had a most melancholy disposition, and so it came as no surprise to the few who knew him that he took his own life."

"I took careful measurements of his approximate height, by means of his clothing, plus the height of the chair that he would have been obliged to stand upon. Allowing for the height of the room, I estimate the length of rope required to hang this man to be no more than four feet."

Gregson reached across his desk to a stack of files that were presumably awaiting removal.

"It was, in fact, less than three," he said after quickly consulting the contents."

"Then the unfortunate Mr Leech would have had to levitate, or jump into the air, in order to place the noose around his neck."

There was silence for a moment, and nothing except a murmur of conversation from the long corridor could be heard.

"I appear to be in error." Gregson's pallor was more bloodless even than usual. "You have seldom been wrong in your assistance in the past, Mr Holmes, so I will re-open the investigation. Can you, perhaps, suggest a motive for this crime?"

"My current client is the occupier of the studio above the rooms of Mr Leech. He has asked me to confirm his suspicions that an intruder has several times entered the studio with the intention of copying his work. I have yet to reach my conclusions, because I believe that there is far more involved here, but of one thing I am certain: Mr Leech was killed to ensure his silence. It is probable that he observed the forger either arriving or leaving, and this tells me at once that more is involved than is at first apparent."

"Is the painting likely to be valuable, then?"

"Not at all. My client, Mr Conk-Singleton, is something of an amateur artist who barely supports himself on his earnings, and the portrait has been specially commissioned by a woman presently visiting here from France."

"All of which has no connection to the murder of Mr Leech unless your theory concerning the intruder is correct," Gregson ventured.

"Quite so. Doubtlessly things will become clearer as my investigation proceeds."

"I wish you well with it, Mr Holmes. As I have said, the death of Abel Leech is now the subject of a murder enquiry, and I trust that you will share with us any information you unearth that could be of help to us. We will pursue this until the truth becomes clear for, as you know, the files here at the Yard are never closed beforehand."

#

We returned to Baker Street with Holmes in a sombre mood. He said little as we spent two hours smoking in our sitting-room before dinner, adopting a contemplative pose as I buried myself in the mid-day edition of *The Standard.* It was after we had eaten and I had poured the last cup from the coffee-pot that he stood up abruptly, gesturing that I should remain seated.

"Remain where you are, old fellow. Enjoy the rest of your coffee. As for me, it is unlikely that I will be returning until late, so pray tell Mrs Hudson that I will need nothing further."

"But Holmes!" I exclaimed as he put on his coat. "Where are you going? If I can be of service I will be glad to accompany you."

"I am about to return to Kirkfield Road, to observe Mr Conk-Singleton's studio until the early hours. If my suppositions are

153

correct, our intruder will favour us with a further visit within the next few days. This will most likely happen when our client has left for his lodgings, but I cannot be sure. For tonight, Watson, I think it best that you stay here to receive any message that Gregson may send, although that does not preclude my having need of your assistance subsequently."

Before I could protest, my friend had turned swiftly away, and I heard him descend the stairs before the door was closed noisily. I moved to the window to see which direction he took, but he procured a hansom immediately and was gone.

I saw nothing of Holmes until the following morning. At breakfast he informed me that his vigil had been cold but uneventful.

"I found a deep doorway almost opposite Mr Conk-Singleton's studio. I knew that my concealment was adequate when he left his premises and passed within a few feet of me, quite unaware of my presence. From then on, apart from the regular appearance of a constable on his beat and two men so sodden with drink that they were unable to walk straight, I saw no one. I think, Watson, that I must spend another night or two in this manner before the forger of our client's work appears."

And so it proved to be. I spent the next three days reading accumulated medical journals that required my attention and, on two occasions, visiting my practice to advise the locum, a young fellow very new to the profession, on the treatment of diseases uncommon in our country.

As Holmes' nightly departure was immediately after dinner, I saw little of him during this time. I assumed that his watchfulness had been so far unrewarded, since he had mentioned nothing of it. Indeed, he had said very little at all.

Finally, I could stand the suspense no longer.

154

"Holmes, has there been any progress at Kirkfield Road?" I enquired as we finished our cheese and potato pie on the fourth evening.

"That was an excellent dinner, Watson," he said with unusual appreciation. "As for your question, the answer is that our adversaries must be becoming increasingly concerned about the delay in the portrait's completion. Every night that passes is therefore more likely than the last to produce a visit from our mysterious forger or Miss Dubois, or perhaps both of them. But I see that you are anxious for the thrill of the game, old friend. Very well, if it is convenient we will keep watch together tonight."

Holmes' anticipation was soon proven correct. We had stood, he in his ear-flapped travelling cap and ulster, in the doorway for some time when our client locked the premises and walked swiftly away. I heard a distant church clock chime the hour of nine o'clock, when an unaccompanied woman appeared and was able to gain entry to the building at once. In the silence we heard her footfalls upon the stairs before the faint light of a candle shone from above.

"Evidently she, too, is proficient with locks," Holmes whispered. "Also she is living nearby, since no hansom or four-wheeler delivered her. Probably she took lodgings that are situated conveniently."

"We could enter the building now," I suggested. "She cannot escape."

"Indeed, there is no way that she could, but my intention is to follow her when she leaves. I wish to know the meaning of this portrait-copying, and why it was necessary to end a man's life to conceal the identities of the intruders. When I give this affair into Gregson's hands it must not be incomplete."

"Holmes, the light has been extinguished!"

No sooner had the faint echo of my words died away than the woman reappeared. After locking the door she set off in the direction from which she had approached, and Holmes and I followed in the shadows. As the streets were empty she apparently thought it unnecessary to ascertain that she walked them alone, for she turned her head not once as she crossed into a dark alley that took her into another thoroughfare from which she turned a corner before ascending the steps of an old house behind metal railings.

We stopped at the corner, using its concealment to observe her destination.

"Meredith Row," Holmes said quietly. "I have been here before."

When the woman had entered and the door had closed we approached the building, and I have no doubt that Holmes would have followed her directly, had not an indistinct figure emerged from behind a cluster of bushes growing in the front garden of a house across the street.

We both were still at once, and my hand closed upon my service revolver in my pocket.

"Good evening, Mr Sherlock Holmes and Doctor Watson," The figure advanced, taking on the shape of a man as it stood briefly under a street lamp. The voice was level and without inflexion or accent.

"Who are you, sir?" I enquired.

He took one step closer. "My name is Garside. My employer is the same as that of your brother, on whose orders I have been maintaining a watch on this house. He anticipated that our paths would cross before long, and requests that you visit him in his chambers tomorrow morning. If you give your name to the attendant, you will be admitted at once."

"By what other name do you know my brother?" Holmes asked.

"His Christian name is 'Mycroft'." In the poor light, I saw the man smile. "Yes, I am genuine, Mr Holmes."

My friend nodded. "Good night then, Mr Garside."

"Goodnight, gentlemen," he replied as we left.

#

We were in Whitehall before nine, the next morning. Holmes had surprised me by making no reference to our encounter with Mr Garside, other than to affirm my availability to accompany him.

"Doubtlessly we will kept waiting until my brother finds a spare moment," he remarked as we approached the building.

"Holmes, I am at a loss to understand the connection between Mycroft and this woman, Marie Dubois."

"It is not yet clear to me, Watson, but I have my suspicions. I do hope that we are about to learn something useful, rather than simply to be told not to interfere in some other affair in which she may be involved."

My friend was wrong, at least, in his prediction of Mycroft's behaviour. The door was opened before us, by a stern-looking man in a morning-suit.

"Good morning, gentlemen. You are expected. Please follow me," he said. Before either of us could say a word, he strode away at a smart pace.

Holmes and I exchanged glances and complied, allowing ourselves to be led down dimly-lit corridors past busts and statues of former members of government. Near a junction with a much wider passage our guide came to an abrupt halt, knocking sharply on a door of panelled oak. On hearing an acknowledgement from within, he bowed and stood aside for us to enter.

The door closed behind us as the elder Holmes rose from behind a large and ornate desk. I barely had time to take in the tall windows and portrait-lined walls of the cavernous room  before he spread his arms in greeting and gestured for us to each take a well-upholstered chair.

"Sherlock," he beamed, "and Doctor Watson. How glad I am to see that you found your way here. I told Garside, only yesterday, that it would not be long before our paths crossed."

As he offered us tea, which we both declined, I noticed that Mycroft had changed little since I saw him last. A little more portly, perhaps, and a few more grey hairs around his temples. His manner was exactly as I remembered.

"It is good to see you, Mycroft, but I am at a loss to understand why we are here," Holmes replied.

"Ah, but of course you would be wondering, dear boy. Let me enlighten you immediately. My people have been watching that house in Kirkfield Road for some little time now, and when you were seen entering I knew at once that the artist fellow who works on the top floor had engaged you. What I need to know is in what capacity, exactly, and whether your activities will in any way interfere with an operation in progress conducted by Her Majesty's Government."

Holmes shrugged his shoulders. "All I can tell you is that the artist, Mr Conk-Singleton, is having difficulty with an unknown intruder who is apparently copying a portrait on which he is currently working. I am to identify the forger and my client will prosecute him. As to why this is taking place and by whom, these things I have yet to discover."

"I believe I can assist you with the answers to both those questions, and then you will see the wider application and importance of this. I can, of course, depend upon the absolute discretion of both you gentlemen?"

There followed a stony silence that lasted for but a few moments. Mycroft had asked us this question before, in this very room, with the same result. Holmes sat, statue-like, staring at his brother angrily.

"Yes, of course," Mycroft said then. I thought I saw a trace of embarrassment in his expression, but it could have been a trick of the light that filtered through the half-closed curtains. He leaned forward in his chair, as if wary of being overheard. "About two months ago one of our clerks, Smith-Harrison, was discovered to have abused his position. He had apparently fallen into that old trap, gambling, and owed a great deal of money to a gaming house in the capital. In order to obtain the necessary funds for repayment, he divulged certain information to a woman who had approached him, we know not how this came to be, as yet. This was Margaret de la Roche, who you know as Marie Dubois. It was she that you were following last night."

"She is some sort of French agent?" I ventured.

"Precisely, Doctor, but not of their government. She is freelance and works internationally, and for the highest bidder. We have been aware for some time of a secret consortium of French arms manufacturers whose objective is to create an immense increase in their profits by initiating a war between their country and ours. Fortunately we have the situation monitored by a group of our people who have slowly infiltrated the inner circle of these rogue industrialists and will inform us as soon as their plan reaches critical proportions. We will then relay the information to Paris and their government will hopefully put paid to the scheme."

The concept of men so inured to the sacredness of human life that they would destroy so much of it for no other purpose than to increase their own wealth appalled me, but I said nothing.

Holmes' face betrayed none of his feelings on the matter.

"Are we to know the nature of the stolen information," he asked.

Mycroft nodded. "A certain phrase was established, in order that our agents would be able to recognise each other, since they were sent out at different times. We are aware that Smith-Harrison divulged this to Mademoiselle de la Roche, or Dubois if you prefer, not that it will do him any good since he has been dealt with and the money impounded."

"Why, I wonder, did this woman not immediately depart for France with the information, or pass it to an accomplice."

"This woman is no amateur, Sherlock," Mycroft explained. "She has become conscious of our observation of her movements. Garside, or one of his colleagues, would report immediately any attempt to travel or to receive visitors who might convey what she has learned elsewhere. My people or Scotland Yard would act at once. In fact, this would have occurred before now, had not my superiors insisted that we stay our hands until we become certain that she is acting alone."

Holmes bowed his head in concentration. "I believe that she has already devised a method of sending this information to her employers," he said. "For why would such a woman as you describe choose a time when she was under close scrutiny by her adversaries to commission a virtually unknown artist to paint her portrait? I think it unlikely that Mr Conk-Singleton is aware of it but he is, in effect, the vehicle that she intends to use to complete her task."

"Something hidden in the portrait, then?" Mycroft enquired.

"Undoubtedly."

"But why are they, whoever they are, copying the picture in our client's studio?" I queried. "Or could it be that he is in error with that assumption?"

Mycroft gave a satisfied smile. "When there are two identical objects, or people for that matter, involved in such circumstances as these, the intention is invariably to substitute one for the other at some point in the proceedings. Would you not agree, Sherlock?"

"I had already reached that conclusion," Holmes confirmed. "It follows that the two portraits are not identical, but have been made to seem so, since the exercise is otherwise pointless. If we may be permitted to pursue our investigation unhindered, Mycroft, I think we may be able to settle this matter to our mutual satisfaction."

The elder Holmes leaned back in his chair and laced his fingers across his ample stomach. "It will do no harm, I suppose, to have a second line of enquiry into this affair. But take care, Sherlock, not to undermine in any way the progress of the official investigation. If you succeed in causing this woman, and any accomplice she may have, to be open to arrest, you will see that I am informed immediately, will you not, dear boy?"

\#

Our hansom was almost back at Baker Street, when Holmes emerged from a silent reverie to direct the driver to halt near a Post Office.

"Have you telegraphed Inspector Gregson?" I asked him as he returned from a short absence.

161

He called for the cabby to drive on. "No, but we will have a visitor, likely this afternoon if it is convenient for him, to ascertain whether our surmise is correct or if our client's portrait has been subjected to alteration."

"You wish to be certain that it is the forgery that contains the information, rather than the original?"

"Precisely. As I have mentioned before, Watson, one must be sure of the facts, before attempting to build upon them."

It was, in fact, a good two hours after we had consumed a luncheon of roast beef with Yorkshire pudding and smoked several pipes, that our door-bell rang.

"Ah, McMasters!" Holmes exclaimed, as Mrs Hudson showed a small, shrew-like man in a top hat and rather worn suit into our sitting-room.

"Always glad to be of service, Mr Holmes," our visitor subserviently assured us.

After introducing me, my friend explained: "Mr McMasters was once the most successful art thief in the capital. When I finally secured his arrest I discovered several extenuating circumstances which I will not elaborate upon now, but suffice it to say that my testimony caused the judge to take a more lenient view than he may have done otherwise."

"And very grateful for that I am too, sir," Mr McMasters affirmed. "I now have a shop where I obtain and sell paintings legally, which brings in less money but leaves me without any fear of the law."

"I am very glad to hear of your redemption," I commented.

"Oh yes, it was that all right. And now, Mr Holmes, how may I assist you today?"

"If you would be so kind as to accompany us to Bethnal Green, there is a portrait that I would like you to inspect. I would be obliged if you would reveal any irregularities or singular features to us."

"That should cause me no great difficulty, sir."

"Capital. It should not take long, I think."

"We do not know if Mr Conk-Singleton will be in his studio, Holmes," I reminded him when we had procured a four-wheeler.

"If he was there earlier, then he will remain until we arrive," my friend said as we turned a sharp corner. "I despatched a telegram to him at the same time as I did so to McMasters."

I said little during the journey, listening instead to the conversation between Holmes and Mr McMasters. I gathered that their connection was from the period shortly after my marriage, when I paid no visits to Baker Street for some time.

We alighted in Kirkfield Road and I paid the driver. The building appeared deserted, but I glanced up and saw our client, clad in a paint-stained smock, move past the window. Holmes opened the door and we took the stairs in single file. The door to the studio was flung open and Mr Conk-Singleton looked down on us.

"Welcome, gentlemen. I trust you have made some advance in your investigation, Mr Holmes?"

"You can be quite certain that we are entering the final chapters of it. Allow me to introduce Mr McMasters, who you will find to have much in common with yourself."

He went on to make the introduction and to explain the purpose of McMasters' presence.

Our client looked annoyed at first, and I supposed this was because he thought himself capable of detecting any alteration to his own work, but the advantage of a fresh pair of knowledgeable eyes must have occurred to him, for he led us further into the studio to where the portrait stood in near-completion.

"Please take care. You will observe that some of the paint is not yet dry."

Mr McMasters gave him a quick glare of disgust, no doubt because such an elementary warning was unnecessary, and proceeded to turn his head this way and that while making little noises of approval and satisfaction. This continued while we watched in silence for about ten minutes, until he turned to us, smiling as he addressed my friend.

"You need have no fears here, Mr Holmes. The brush strokes are clear and consistent, the colours without variation. I would stake my reputation – no, my life, that no other hand save that of the artist has laid a brush to that canvas."

"Excellent. My thanks to you, McMasters. Perhaps you would care to accompany Doctor Watson downstairs, where he will call you a hansom to return you to your shop."

When this was done I returned to the studio to find Holmes reporting to Mr Conk-Singleton.

"I am certain therefore," he said, "that a similar examination, applied to the forgery, will reveal to us the purpose of all this."

Our client nodded his head. "But how will we acquire the copy?"

"Is the genuine portrait now completed?"

"I have delayed finishing it, as you previously suggested, but this has become increasingly difficult as I worked upon it. As it is now, I could give it the final touches within an hour."

Holmes let his eyes wander around the room, looking thoughtful. I knew from of old that his mind was racing.

"Very well," he said at last. "The time has come to lay the hidden aspects of this case bare. Have you received any indication as to Miss Dubois' next visit?"

"Not at all. As I mentioned before, she now appears unannounced."

"Indeed. If you will follow my instructions exactly, I believe we can settle this soon."

"I will do as you direct, Mr Holmes. I now have other commissions that I am anxious to begin to fulfil."

"Excellent. When Miss Dubois next appears, I want you to confirm to her that the portrait is complete. Tell her also that it has not turned out as well as you hoped and you are disappointed. Accordingly, say that you intend to destroy it the following morning, and that she owes you nothing. I anticipate that she will be outraged of course, will entreat you to reconsider and perhaps offer you an increased payment. If you wish to discover the truth of all this you must stand firm, because everything is dependent upon her leaving here without the portrait. The only other thing you must do is to wire me immediately before returning to your lodgings until I send for you."

Mr Conk-Singleton had looked dejected at the mention of the destruction of his work, but now his face brightened. "This I will do, whenever Miss Dubois chooses to make her final visit."

"We will be waiting to hear from you. Come Watson, I see that a hansom has discharged its fare across the street."

#

The next five days occupied Holmes with a case that I have recorded and entitled 'The Adventure of the Bishop's Nightmare', and which has been consigned to my despatch box at Cox & Co until such time as my friend consents to its release. I took little part in it because of several emergencies which confronted me at my practice, but my friend narrated the details at its conclusion. At the end of this time we were sitting before a roaring fire in our sitting-room enjoying our after-dinner pipes, until the door-bell rang and Mrs Hudson laid a yellow envelope before Holmes.

He tore the contents free of their covering, and his expression lightened at once.

"At last! Watson, it is the expected wire from Mr Conk-Singleton. By the time we reach his studio it will be fully dark, which will aid our purpose." He smiled. "It will be satisfying to reflect that I have solved two cases in one day."

At Holmes' direction, the cabby left us some distance from 37 Kirkfield Road. Shortly afterwards we stood, concealed by shadows, for fully five minutes before he was sure that the building was unobserved.

"I wanted to be certain," he explained, "not only that Garside or another of Mycroft's people were not nearby (they would probably be concentrating still on Meredith Row) but also that Miss Dubois and her associates had not become suspicious. I have seen to it that Gregson has been informed, and I suppose I am duty bound to disclose the outcome of this to my brother if all goes well."

At that we approached the building and gained entrance by his use of his pick-lock. I closed the door behind us with a faint echo and we ascended the stairs with care.

"No lights, Watson, we cannot risk even a candle," he whispered. "I trust you have your service revolver?"

"My hand is upon it at this moment," I replied quietly as we opened the door.

In the darkness the studio looked enormous. It was lit faintly by the light from the window and skylights, and the atmosphere was thick with the smell of paint and spirit. The raucous laughter of some passers-by reached us from the street and occasional hansoms or landaus were heard briefly, but otherwise we waited in silence.

Gradually the activity outside dwindled, before ceasing altogether. Now only the distant chimes of the church clock broke into our separate thoughts. We had stood, unmoving for almost three hours when I felt Holmes grip my arm and lean close.

"They are here, Watson," he whispered. "Make no sound and remain still until they are within our grasp."

Then I heard what his keen ears had already. A scrabbling and scratching as the lock to the outer door was turned, far more clumsily than when my friend had opened it previously. There was an audible curse in a foreign language, and then cautious footfalls on the stairs.

The door opened to admit two figures, their shapes indistinct in the darkness. From the quick exchange in French, too fast for me to follow but Holmes doubtlessly understood, it became apparent that they were a man and a woman. For a moment all was still, then the man lit an oil lamp in the same instant that Holmes stepped sideways, barring their retreat.

"Good evening, Miss Dubois, or should I say Mademoiselle de la Roche?" They froze instantly, appearing shocked by our presence. "And you sir are, I think, Monsieur Jules Claudell, who is wanted by the French police for art theft and forgery."

The man recovered himself quickly, and placed the lamp on a side-table.

"And who are you, sir? An agent of the English police, I imagine."

His speech was so heavily accented that I found it hard to understand. Holmes, however, had no such difficulty.

"Not at all. My name is Sherlock Holmes."

"That name means nothing to me."

"Possibly not, but I see from the change in your companion's expression that she recognises it."

Miss Dubois launched into a tirade of rapid French and Monsieur Claudell inclined his head to listen. She was evidently explaining to him who they were dealing with, for he brushed his hand across his short beard in a nervous gesture.

"So, but we are caught, all the same." He reached slowly into the case he carried, and I produced my service revolver at once.

"Thank you Watson," Holmes responded. "I would be obliged, Monsieur Claudell, if you would refrain from extracting that paint-knife from your bag. I am sure you are as adept at throwing it as you would be if it were a weapon designed for that purpose, and I have no desire to be used as a pin-cushion."

The Frenchman dropped the bag to the floor.

"What do you want with us?" Miss Dubois asked in an affronted manner. "We have committed no crime that you can prove, and you have no authority to detain us."

Holmes raised his eyebrows. "If you do not consider art forgery a crime, possibly because neither the artist nor his work are famous, you will certainly acknowledge that murder falls within that description. As for my authority, it is no more than that of an ordinary law-abiding citizen, but I think it is time that we summoned the official force regarding these matters. Watson, pray be so kind as to pass me your revolver."

I did this cautiously, since this action provided our prisoners with a momentary opportunity to gain the upper hand. They made no such attempt however, and Holmes pointed the weapon in their direction as he reached into his pocket without averting his eyes.

"Here is a police whistle, Watson. I would be obliged if you would go down into the street and use it. Unless I am much mistaken, I believe that you will find that Inspector Gregson and one or two constables are close at hand."

I complied instantly, and reflected that Holmes must have warned Gregson of the anticipated situation, since he and two uniformed police officers appeared almost at once from the shadows further along the street. In the studio, nothing further had occurred.

"Ah, Gregson!" Holmes exclaimed as we re-joined him. "These are the two I mentioned in my wire. Whether one or both of them murdered Mr Abel Leech I am uncertain, but you will doubtlessly be able to ascertain the truth of it when they are in custody."

"Thank you, Mr Holmes," the Scotland Yard man replied as he looked the prisoners over. "It will be good to close the file on this matter. It never sits well with me to leave loose ends." He gestured to one of his companions. "Take them out, Noakes."

The constables had almost reached the door with their charges, when Holmes turned suddenly, as if he had recalled an unsettled aspect of the case.

"One moment!" He addressed the prisoners once more, after retrieving Monsieur Claudell's portrait from the bag which lay at his feet. "Presumably, you intended to effect the exchange tonight. Perhaps you would care to explain the purpose or significance of the second portrait," he glanced at the picture displayed on the easel, "for it is very nearly identical. Come, it cannot matter to you now. Why did you, Miss Dubois, not simply take Mr Conk-Singleton's work for Monsieur Claudell to alter, before returning to your masters in France?"

She related my friend's words to her companion, who replied only with a crafty smile, before replying.

"That is for you to discover, Mr Holmes, if you can."

Gregson glanced through the window. "The transportation that I ordered has arrived, I see. These two will be in the cells within the hour, and we will see if they are so flippant then. We will leave you now, gentlemen, with our thanks once again."

We watched from the window as the police coach, with the prisoners safely manacled inside, began its journey back to the Yard. Holmes secured the premises and we walked to the end of the street before we were fortunate enough to encounter a passing landau.

Shortly afterwards we were back in our lodgings, enjoying a glass of brandy before retiring. After removing both portraits from Monsieur Claudell's bag which he had brought with him, Holmes placed them on the hearth, side by side.

"As you see, Watson, it is only a detail in the background that is different." With a long finger he indicated a group of trees, which differed slightly on the forgery. "You will recall that Mycroft mentioned that Miss Dubois had induced one of his staff to divulge a recognition signal to her, in exchange for payment, so we must proceed with the assumption that it is that which is hidden somewhere here. But I perceive that you are weary, old fellow. I suggest that you retreat to your room while I attempt to make some sense of this, and allow yourself a good night's rest. No, do not concern yourself regarding me. I am no stranger to remaining awake until morning, as you know, and I am quite determined that the solution to this little puzzle will not elude me. Good night, and I hope to be able to throw some light upon this at breakfast."

Surprisingly, I slept well, and did not dream at all. I emerged rather late into our sitting-room to find Holmes in fine form, looking as alert as ever and about to begin his consumption of a plate of bacon and eggs. He immediately called for Mrs Hudson to serve me similarly.

"You look amazingly unaffected by the loss of a night's sleep, if I may say so, Holmes."

"That, my dear Watson, is because I slept almost as long as yourself."

"Ah, you were too tired after all, to attempt to decipher whatever is hidden in the picture. A wise decision, things always seem easier when you confront them with a mind that is fresh."

He laughed shortly. "You misunderstand me, old fellow. Pah! The puzzle was a simple one, after all. I tried several numerical ciphers that I am familiar with, based on the number of trees painted in the background of the forgery and the irregularity of their spacing, but it was not until the fifth application that I finally discovered the key. After that I went to my bed and slept, only about an hour after you had retired."

"You never cease to amaze me, " I said truthfully. "The only thing that I am still not clear about is your question to Miss Dubois, of early this morning. Why did they need to involve Mr Conk-Singleton at all? Why did she not allow Monsieur Claudell to paint the picture from the outset? Or, as you put it then, why did she not take the finished portrait to Monsieur Claudell to be altered after Mr Conk-Singleton had completed it?"

"That had already occurred to me," he glanced at his pocket watch. "I therefore wired Gregson a little earlier, requesting that he asked those two beauties the same question. It may be that they have become more amenable, by this time. Ah, I hear the door-bell now, and Mrs Hudson has delayed bringing our coffee while she answers. I shall be surprised if she does not bring us a telegram in a few minutes."

He was, of course, correct. Our good landlady brought in a pot of steaming coffee and laid a yellow envelope before him. While I poured for us both he extracted the form and glanced over its contents.

"There is no mystery here, Watson," he said with an air of disappointment as he placed the message within my reach.

I read it and understood at once. Both Miss Dubois and Monsieur Claudell were aware that they were under observation by Mycroft's people. They were both notorious in their own fields of subterfuge, and so this was nothing new to them. Had they attempted to dispatch the portrait, by any medium, to France, it would have been immediately intercepted. They resolved therefore to involve Mr Conk-Singleton, and on completion of his work they would make the substitution without his knowledge before Miss Dubois requested him to effect the picture's transportation, no

172

doubt giving some excuse as to why she was unable to do this personally. There was indeed, no mystery.

Holmes' mood had changed. He appeared suddenly downcast, frowning as he regarded his untouched coffee.

"I congratulate you," I said lightly. "Again you have succeeded where Scotland Yard failed."

"But I have derived little satisfaction from it." He glanced toward the window. "It seems certain that it will rain soon, Watson, but I feel that a brisk walk would be beneficial. Bring your umbrella, old fellow, and who knows? By the time we return a more interesting problem may well have presented itself."

The Adventure of the Grand Vizier

During my long and extraordinary association with my friend, Mr Sherlock Holmes, we shared many adventures of a nature that I could easily have accepted as having a supernatural, or somewhat unearthly, basis. He, however, would have none of that, always maintaining that every event, no matter how unexplainable or unusual it seemed, would be found in the end to have a perfectly ordinary and logical explanation. Some situations, as my friend was always pleased to point out, were made to appear to be products of the occult or something contrary to natural laws quite deliberately, in order to bring about circumstances that would profit the perpetrator of the delusion.

As I search my despatch box, to unearth such a tale at my publisher's request, I find myself drawn to the documented description of one of my friend's cases that has long been overlooked, in favour of the more dramatic incidents that have built his well-deserved reputation.

It was, as I remember, a fine autumn day that found me enjoying my first pipe after breakfast as I immersed myself in the early edition of *The Standard*. Holmes stood gazing down from the window, his face expressionless and his cigar unlit.

"What has arrested your attention in Baker Street, Holmes?" I asked after a few moments, lowering my newspaper.

He replied without averting his gaze. "I am observing the antics of a most indecisive fellow. Apart from the fact that he appears to be in great fear of something, I can make nothing of him. He has three times made to cross between the passing

174

hansoms to our door, and three times altered his intention at the last moment."

"Is he perhaps pursued by someone from whom he wishes to conceal his destination?"

My friend shook his head. "Unlikely I think, Watson. I have been watching him for at least five minutes, and he has not as much as looked around him or behind him. No, he is suffering an internal conflict over whether or not to consult us, which suggests that the matter is something of which he is embarrassed or uncertain."

I returned my attention to the newspaper. "Doubtlessly you will tell me, if he decides to visit us."

"Aha!" Holmes cried. "I think he has come to consider us as his best course of action. Whatever his difficulty may be, we are to get the opportunity to assist him. The door-bell will ring within the next thirty seconds, Watson, since he has run headlong between a hansom and a landau in his efforts to arrive on our doorstep."

As always, my friend was correct. Mrs Hudson must have been nearby, since the door was opened before the final peal had died away. We then heard hurried footsteps upon the stairs before she opened our door for the man to enter.

"Mr Randolph Pindler to see Mr Holmes," she announced. "I will serve tea in a moment, gentlemen."

"Well anticipated, Mrs Hudson. Thank you."

Mr Pindler stood looking confused. His eyes went from Holmes to myself then back again. I concluded that he was in a frantic state.

My friend rose and approached him. "I am Sherlock Holmes and this is my friend and colleague Doctor John Watson. I see that you are suffering some anxiety, which I am certain that we will be able to dispel. There is a slight chill in the air, is there not? The chair on your right, nearest the fire, you will find to be most comfortable. Pray be seated."

I fancied that I saw Mr Pindler tremble slightly as he took his seat. A small man, clean-shaven except for a rather unkempt moustache, he carried no hat and wore a pea-coat that had evidently seen much service.

"Thank you, Gentlemen," he said in a wavering voice. "I do not know how yourselves, or indeed anyone, can throw any light on my strange experience of last night, but if you will hear my story you will at least understand why it is that you see me in such a fearful state."

"Do not distress yourself on that point," my friend replied. "Many fantastical accounts have been heard in this room, but few have remained so after some little investigation. Proceed, please, for you have our undivided attention."

The little man shifted in his seat. "Well, gentlemen, to begin I should explain that I am the night watchman of the Egyptian Gallery at the British Museum. Recently the mummy of a man, not a Pharaoh I think, was added to the exhibits. There was little left of it, so it was displayed upright in a glass case rather than enclosed in an ornate coffin as is usual. Last night, as I completed my first rounds, I noticed that another exhibit that has been on display for some months now was missing from its place. It was the fabled Sceptre of Anubis, and I had hardly recovered from the shock of its absence when I heard footsteps approaching along the adjoining corridor. Thinking that this must be Mr Thomas Glowry, the curator who occasionally calls in unexpectedly at all hours, I rushed to meet him at once to tell him of my discovery, but I was completely unprepared for what confronted me as I turned a corner."

"What could it have been," I asked him, "that has caused you such distress?"

Our visitor's voice rose almost to a shriek. "It was the mummy, sirs, the one I mentioned. I swear to you that it was walking down the passageway with the Sceptre of Anubis held before it, as if intending to make an offering of it to the gods."

At that moment, after knocking, the door opened to reveal Mrs Hudson laden with the tea tray. I took it from her and thanked her, and she withdrew after a curious glance at our guest.

After I had poured each of us a cup, Holmes held up a bottle of brandy.

"I believe that a little of this in your tea will help to calm you, Mr Pindler", he said before adding some to the beverage.

"Why thank you, sir, I'm sure it will."

In less than five minutes the cups were all returned to the tray, and our visitor did indeed seem to have regained himself somewhat.

"My dear Mr Pindler," Holmes began. "Whatever else might be discovered during our investigations, I assure you now that a living mummy will not feature in it. The dead remain dead sir, no matter for how long. Clearly then, you have been subjected to some sort of trickery. Pray tell us of your actions immediately after witnessing this extraordinary sight."

Our guest became downcast at once. "I lost my senses as the apparition drew nearer. I am ashamed to say that I have always been prone to such a weakness. I fainted dead away like a schoolgirl."

"Which, I have no doubt, is exactly what was intended, so that the stealer of the Sceptre could escape unobserved. You see what we have learned already, that the person responsible knew that you would be on duty alone, is aware of the value or significance of the Sceptre and that you are of a nervous disposition. Therefore, he reasoned, because of this last some sort of shock was necessary in order to remove you as an obstacle. No, it is not to the realms of the supernatural that we should look here, rather to those who are familiar with both you and the museum. A colleague, possibly, I think."

"You dispel my fears so effortlessly, Mr Holmes," Mr Pindler looked distinctly brighter. "But I fear that there is something else."

"Then kindly elaborate."

"The curator, Mr Thomas Glowry, suspects me of taking the Sceptre. Inspector Lestrade of Scotland Yard was called in this morning, and he gave me the same impression."

"Other than the fact that you were present during the robbery, have they any other reason for believing this?"

Mr Pindler averted his eyes. "Yes sir, I'm afraid they have. Five years ago I was convicted of stealing from a baker's shop where I worked in those days. My wife and child were starving sir, we could not pay our rent and live on the pittance I earned. I took two or three loaves of bread, and we hadn't had a mouthful each before the constables arrived. My family died while I was in prison, but after my release I managed to find this job at the museum, where I've worked ever since. Mr Glowry knew of this when he took me on, he gave me a chance that he will be regretting now."

Holmes and I murmured our condolences at our visitor's double loss.

"Very well," my friend said after a moment of thought. "We will see what can be done. You have only to disclose to us any details that you may know about this mummy, and then I think we need to detain you no further. You can be assured that we will spare no effort to get to the bottom of this curious affair."

Mr Pindler's relief was evident. "I will tell you all I know, gentlemen, but I fear that it is very little. The mummy is always referred to as that of Em-Todeh, and it was discovered during an excavation three years ago at a place called el-Amarra. The Egyptologist who led the expedition was Sir Oswald Hendrie."

#

Luncheon that day was Mrs Hudson's excellent shepherd's pie, of which I ate the greater part. Holmes consumed his share mechanically, his mind elsewhere. When I at last laid my knife and fork upon my soiled plate, awareness returned to his eyes.

"We can be at the British Museum within the hour, Watson." He rose and glanced down from the window. "Be a good fellow and pass me my hat and coat."

We had no difficulty in securing a hansom, and alighted at our destination after a journey that Holmes spent deep in thought. We had made no arrangements for an interview with Mr Thomas Lowry, and had impressed upon our client that he should ignore our presence if he was recalled to the premises on the instructions of Scotland Yard. It appeared as if Inspector Lestrade had already concluded his investigation, for there was no sign of him or his men.

We made our way through rooms of natural history, through galleries of skeletal remains of animals that once roamed the Earth and those that still inhabited places far away. After passing through an array of armour, weapons and many insights into civilisations long past, we came upon a square room bedecked with Ancient Egyptian discoveries. All signs of activity had gone, and we were quite alone in there.

Holmes stood quite still, his eyes taking in the death masks and mummy caskets surrounding us. After a moment he walked slowly around the perimeter, staring intently at the floor.

"It has been many a century, Watson, since such as these walked the Earth. I take it that this vacant plinth is where the mummy of Em-Todeh formerly stood."

I peered at the panel nearby. "That is correct, Holmes."

He then whipped out his lens, carefully examining the floor and crawling on his hands and knees towards the exit.

"Aha!" he cried. "Much of it has been disturbed and swept away by Lestrade's clod-footed blunderers, but still traces remain."

"What have you discovered?"

"The remains of the wrongly accused, I think." He produced an envelope from his pocket and proceeded to scrape a tiny quantity of a fine brown leaf into it.

"That is from the body of Em-Todeh?"

"Probably. I shall confirm it later. He is hardly in a condition to steal anything and walk around with it, wouldn't you say?"

"It seems to me that there must be very little left of him. But what was it then, than Mr Pindler saw?"

"We will get to that shortly. For now, let us attempt to follow this hardly visible trail to its conclusion."

He then got to his feet, bending low so that he could continue to see the floor with his lens as he crossed the room to a corner. An unmarked door stood before us and he looked around for assistance from any museum staff within earshot. Seeing none, he called out twice. We waited, but no response was forthcoming. Holmes gave a slight shrug and produced his pick-lock. The door was opened in seconds.

"The mummy's destination is revealed, Watson," Holmes announced, "but the fate of the Sceptre is still to be determined."

I looked past him into what was little more than an alcove, apparently used for storage. The crumbling remains of Em-Todeh lay in a heap in a corner. Holmes bent to examine them but stood up more quickly than I expected, to transfer his attention to a bundle of brown paper that had been crushed into a ball and forced into a sack.

"Who has done this, Holmes?"

"That we will doubtless discover, but you see what has occurred here? The thief removed the remains of Em-Todeh, leaving a trail of his crumbling body leading to this cupboard, where he hid them. His purpose, I am sure, was to take his place on the plinth until Mr Pindler's rounds were completed and the opportunity presented itself for him to abscond with the Sceptre of Anubis."

"But," I protested, "how could anyone adopt such a disguise?"

"This happened during the hours of darkness, did it not?"

"During the night, according to Mr Pindler."

"And, as I am sure you have noticed, at least half the gas lamps in this gallery have been tampered with. It would have been a very shadowy form that our client saw, if indeed he did see it before the encounter in the corridor after the theft."

"Mr Pindler did not mention the lamps."

"He was overwhelmed by what he had witnessed. He would surely have reported it to his superiors, otherwise."

"So how do we proceed, Holmes?"

He consulted his pocket-watch. "It is getting late, and the museum will close soon. I suggest we return to Baker Street, where I am sure we will find that Mrs Hudson has prepared for us an excellent dinner."

#

We ate our roast pork and apple sauce with relish, I more than he, as is often the case. He did little justice to the following treacle steamed pudding.

No sooner had Mrs Hudson cleared away the plates and cutlery, than he began chemical experiments on the scarred table that he used for the purpose. I retired to my armchair with a glass of brandy and a newly-arrived medical journal until he emerged and sat near the unlit fire.

"How was it, old fellow?" I asked.

"Much as I expected. The powdery substance from the museum floor was indeed part of the remnants of both the mummy and its wrappings, so it would appear that my reconstruction of the theft was accurate."

"But where does that lead us to? Are we to interview the museum staff tomorrow?"

He considered this. "Later, perhaps. First I would like to know more about both this ancient Egyptian and the Sceptre of Anubis. I recall that Mr Pindler mentioned that the Egyptologist who discovered the tomb of Em-Todeh was Sir Oswald Hendrie, during an expedition of three years ago. Be a good fellow and look him up for me. Our copy of *Who's Who* is just above your left shoulder. His address will be sufficient."

I put down my brandy glass and picked up the volume. "Eleven, Cheam Passage," I quoted.

"Which is just off Berkeley Square, as I recall. Very well, we will pay Sir Oswald a visit after breakfast. As for tonight, I will join you in a glass of brandy as we discuss some of the previous cases that you have persistently enquired about lately. Afterwards I suggest that we retire early, for tomorrow is likely to be busy for us."

Holmes was finishing his breakfast with a slice of buttered toast as I joined him. His expression told me that he had given our current case much thought already and I, also, had ceased to eat before he emerged from his distraction.

"Drink your coffee, Watson. I think you will find that it has now cooled sufficiently. We will need to make other calls after we have spoken with Sir Oswald."

Cheam Passage proved to be a row of identical houses with pillared porticos in white stone, near Berkeley Square as Holmes had said. I paid off the hansom and we approached the door numbered eleven after casting our eyes around us. Our surroundings were deserted and the only sound was of distant traffic.

Holmes rapped upon the door, which was answered quickly by an elderly white-haired man with the most elaborate moustache That I have ever seen.

"Pray tell me," said my friend, "is Sir Oswald Hendrie at home?"

The old man smiled. "Indeed he is, for I am he. I live alone you see, I have no need of servants." He stretched out a tanned arm to shake hands with Holmes. "And you are Mr Sherlock Holmes, I think, and your companion will be Doctor Watson. I have read with great interest of your exploits, which I find almost as fascinating as the mysteries of Ancient Egypt." He shook my hand with equal enthusiasm, before stepping aside to let us pass. "But come in, sirs, come in."

We entered a spacious room with laden bookshelves on every wall. As I had expected, there were souvenirs of Sir Oswald's expeditions all around. When we were seated in the leather armchairs that surrounded a highly-polished table he offered us port, which we both declined at this early hour. He poured himself a large glass but left it untouched, seemingly eager for conversation.

"I get few visitors these days, gentlemen, other than fellow Egyptologists now and then. My brief moments of fame have passed, and I am largely forgotten. But I have my memories and my books, and the freedom to walk around London if I wish, so I am content." His glance fell briefly on a folded newspaper upon the table. "I have read in *The London Gazette* that there has been some trouble at the British Museum involving the mummy I brought back from the el-Amarra expedition. Presumably, that is why you have called?"

"Indeed," Holmes replied, "and the Sceptre of Anubis has disappeared in most extraordinary circumstances. In order for me to begin an investigation, it is necessary for me to know something of the background of both the Sceptre and the mummy of Em-Todeh. Both Doctor Watson and myself would be most grateful for any assistance from you in this matter."

184

"Yes, I see." Sir Oswald let his head fall onto his chest for a moment, as he collected his thoughts. "First I must explain that el-Amarra was the capital established by Akenhaten, the so-called 'heretic Pharaoh'. He was the ruler who rejected the traditional Egyptian gods in favour of a single deity – Aten. Em-Todeh, as far as we can tell from our studies of the remnants of various hieroglyphics – painted on tomb walls and similar surfaces around the site, you understand – was one of a number of high-ranking officers in the Pharaoh's court, probably what we would recognise as a grand vizier, or equivalent rank. The Sceptre of Anubis was a ceremonial tool already ancient around 1340BC, the period of Akenhaten's rule."

"Has its significance been established?" I asked.

The old man's face lit up. "It has, and I am not boasting when I say that I, myself, played a large part in that. The inscriptions, when translated, revealed that the Sceptre was traditionally believed to be the key used by Anubis, the god of the underworld, to unlock the way to transport the Pharaoh into the afterlife. One of the mysteries attached to all this is how it came to be in the court of Akenhaten, who believed only in a single god. It is generally supposed that it was allowed there exceptionally for another person, possibly a concubine."

"So Em-Todeh was made the official guardian of the Sceptre?" Holmes enquired.

"Indeed. He was charged to protect it from all harm, with his life if necessary, in this world and the next."

"My thanks to you, Sir Oswald. Just one more question, if you please, then we will disturb you no longer."

Our host nodded. "Of course. Please continue."

185

"Is the Sceptre of monetary value, that is to say valuable to a common thief? Could such a thief dispose of it as he would, for example, stolen pearls or diamonds?"

Sir Oswald seemed surprised at this. "Good heavens, sir, no. It is true that the Sceptre is inlaid with coloured stones, but these are not such as we consider valuable. They are merely for decoration and would not be worthy of appraisal. The value of the Sceptre lies entirely within its historical concept, and is meaningless except to those who appreciate the treasures of history. I recall a similar discussion with Mr Thomas Glowry, the museum curator."

Holmes and I rose as one, to shake hands again with Sir Oswald.

"My thanks to you again, sir." Holmes repeated as we left. "You have thrown much light on this matter."

#

We hailed a hansom shortly after emerging from Berkeley Square. Holmes seemed rather pleased with the interview. The frown which often dominated his features in the midst of a case was, I noticed, entirely absent.

"It went well, then." I remarked, to encourage him to speak.

"It was satisfactory."

"But what, apart from some interesting history, did we actually learn, Holmes?"

"The essence of the entire conversation was concentrated on my final question."

"I cannot follow your reasoning."

He turned from observing the passing scene. "We now know that our robber moves within circles other than those of the common criminal. Only someone who appreciates the historical value of the Sceptre would have gone to such trouble to possess it. Also, my original suspicion that someone connected with the museum and Egyptology is confirmed, for what would a commonplace thief want with something he could not dispose of profitably? Sir Oswald stated as much – the Sceptre has no value except to someone who appreciates its historical significance. We are looking for a collector of sorts, I think."

We alighted near the entrance to the British Museum. Once inside, Holmes turned away from the corridor leading to the displays and exhibits, following instead a narrow passage that brought us to a number of storerooms and offices. We came to an abrupt halt before a door on which was proclaimed, in ornate script, the name of the Museum Curator.

My friend opened the door carefully, to reveal a chamber lined with bookshelves and pictures of historical or natural significance. A small desk with a typewriting machine, presumably used by a secretary, stood empty to our left. The man sitting at the much larger desk to our right stared at us, surprised at our sudden entry.

"I fear you have taken a wrong turn, gentlemen," he intoned in a hoarse voice. "The public rooms are entered by means of the adjacent corridor."

"Not so, Mr Thomas Glowry," my friend replied. "Or purpose here is to see you."

"I was not aware that I had an appointment."

"There was no appointment. We are here to put things to rights."

Mr Glowry showed a flicker of interest. "Who are you, sir?"

"My name is Sherlock Holmes. My companion is Doctor John Watson."

"Ah, the thieftaker. I have read of you occasionally. What does this supposed wrong that you speak of, concern?"

"The theft of the Sceptre of Anubis."

"You have recovered it?" he asked hopefully.

"Not yet, but I believe I am close to doing so."

Mr Glowry sighed, and moved awkwardly in his chair. Against the wall behind him leaned a heavy wooden crutch, and I knew that Holmes also would have concluded that the man was a cripple.

"Very well. Pray be seated, and we will discuss the matter."

We settled ourselves in the upright chairs in front of his desk, and I studied the man as we did so. Mr Thomas Lowry was a tall, heavy-set man with a sombre expression. His hair was black with the first signs of grey visible and he was clean-shaven except for his side-whiskers, which he had allowed to grow down to his jawbone. His clothes were worn but of good taste.

"I must tell you, gentlemen," he informed us at once, "that the thief is known to me as someone who is employed here. The only reason that he is not at this moment in the hands of Scotland Yard is that I cannot prove his dishonesty, for I am unable, in good conscience, to condemn him on mere suspicion. However, this man has before now been convicted of a crime, and it is difficult to see how anyone else could be responsible. He was alone in the museum at the time of the theft in the course of his duties, and seeks to excuse himself with fantastical excuses. I have no doubts that Inspector Lestrade will form the same conclusion, and that will be the end of it."

Holmes had listened intently. "Very much to the contrary, sir. I think the good inspector will absolve Mr Randolph Pindler, if he has not already. Although my investigation is not yet complete, I have established to my satisfaction that he is quite innocent of any wrongdoing. He appreciates that you employed him knowing of his past, and would never consider jeopardising his income."

"But what of his ridiculous story?" Mr Glowry was clearly surprised that Holmes did not concur with his understanding of events. "Surely, Mr Holmes, you are not of the belief that the mummy of a man dead since ancient times can arise and walk off with one of our exhibits to heaven-knows-where?"

"Not at all. But to Mr Pindler this appeared to happen. I have already ascertained how it was done. His delicate nervous state played an essential part in the plan, for little strain was required to induce a fainting spell."

"You astonish me, sir." The curator shook his head in bewilderment.

"To your knowledge, Mr Glowry, have any others taken an undue interest in the Sceptre of Anubis," I asked. "Perhaps someone has visited the display on unusually numerous occasions?"

"Excellent, Watson," I heard Holmes mutter beside me.

After some small consideration, Mr Glowry explained. "There have been some visitors who came out of curiosity to see Em-Todeh, there usually is with any new exhibit. We had a few parents with schoolchildren, but on the whole the response had been disappointing. Egyptology is a fascination only to some, outside of those with knowledge of the subject or with a passion for it." He shook his head in a hopeless gesture. "The most frequent visitors of course, are members of past expeditions and lecturers, and a young fellow from the British Egyptological Society."

I sensed a quickening of Holmes' movements. He leaned forward in his chair, his eyes glittering.

"And who is that, pray?"

"Oh, our regular student of all things Egyptian, Mr Lionel Watting. I do not think you need concern yourself with him, Mr Holmes, for he has not attended lately and his connection with the museum is of long standing."

My friend rose and I followed.

"As I have stated, Mr Glowry, my enquiries are as yet unfinished. I have every reason to expect a satisfactory conclusion before too long. I thank you, sir, for allowing us this interview."

After that I can recall only a hurried shaking of hands before we found ourselves once more in the streets of London.

"Is our next call to be on this fellow Watting, Holmes?" I enquired as we awaited a hansom.

"Most likely, but first I must consult my index. It is, in any case, nearing the time for luncheon, and I recall that Mrs Hudson was in the process of baking a chicken and ham pie as we left earlier. I am sure that it will satisfy you until dinner, Watson."

Holmes went straight to his scrapbooks on our arrival at Baker Street, treating our luncheon as a momentary diversion from his purpose. As I consumed my own meal and the stewed apple that followed, I watched him as he kneeled to turn pages and dismiss their contents impatiently.

"Ha!" he cried triumphantly. "I knew the name was familiar to me."

I left the table to peer over my friend's shoulder. He held a cutting from the *Evening Standard* of a few months earlier, with an indistinct picture of a thin young man holding a stone sculpture of a cat.

"At any rate, Holmes, it seems that this Lionel Watting is exactly who he represents himself to be. He is indeed a regular visitor to the British Museum, in one capacity or another."

"I had expected nothing different."

"Do you believe him to be somehow involved in this?"

"I suspect so, but I will be certain only when we have seen him." Without replacing his scrapbooks he got to his feet and took up his hat and coat. "Come, Watson, I feel that we are nearing the end of this affair."

He must have obtained an address from his index, for he had no hesitation in directing the driver of the four-wheeler that he summoned as it passed. I saw that we were travelling north, eventually passing through Harrow, into increasingly rural surroundings. After several farms were left behind we turned into a well-kept park, the edge of an estate I discerned, but our conveyance came to halt near a long low building of impressive design that stood some distance from the main house. Holmes requested the driver to wait, and we both noticed the movement of the curtains as we approached the single entrance.

"I do not anticipate a friendly reception here, Watson," he said as he rapped upon the door with his cane.

He was immediately proven correct, as the door was flung open to reveal the young man who had featured in the photograph.

His expression was hostile and his jaw held rigid in an aggressive stance.

"I know you, you are Holmes the busybody detective. Why are you here? I should tell you that you are trespassing on the estate of Lord Galtacre, and that I am under his protection."

My friend's expression remained unaltered. "I am flattered that you have heard of me. It is of no surprise that his Lordship protects you, since you evidently reside upon his property. However, we are here to request your assistance in recovering the stolen Sceptre of Anubis."

"I have heard of that icon in the course of my Egyptological studies, but never laid eyes on it." Mr Watting spluttered, his face reddening with obvious guilt. "Whatever has befallen it is no concern of mine."

"Come now," Holmes said reasonably. "You cannot claim to be innocent in the face of so much evidence to the contrary. All is known. I doubt that Lord Galtacre will appreciate being dragged into the scandal that will surely result, if you do not take advantage of this chance to put matters right. You will find that it is far easier to deal with me than Scotland Yard."

The young man's angry expression was replaced by a furtive look. "What do you imagine that you have against me? There is no proof that I have committed any crime."

"You may well think that, but my entire strategy is without fault. It is based upon the fact that your preferred newspaper is *The London Morning News*."

"Such impeccable reasoning," Mr Watting replied sarcastically. "If that is the extent of your perception, then clearly I have nothing to fear. It might interest you to know that the only newspaper I ever read is *The Times*."

The door was slammed in our faces, but Holmes wore a grim smile as we returned to the hansom. We were well on our way back to Baker Street, before I asked:

"What is this evidence that you have against Mr Watting, Holmes? I was completely unaware of it."

"Apart from what we have just learned, there is the bandage on his left wrist, and the tiny remnants of the mummy from the museum floor adhering to his boots."

"I confess to learning nothing except the name of the newspaper he takes."

" I deliberately stated another, and he was kind enough to correct me. I fear that Mr Watting has not proven to be a very worthwhile adversary."

I looked out into the street, my attention attracted by the cries of a group of urchins begging outside a bakery.

"I can make nothing of any of this," I admitted, turning to face him.

"Then," he said patiently, "cast your mind back to when we discovered the remains of Em-Todeh's mummy, at the British Museum. Do you recall that anything else had been left in the same place?"

"Surely, there was nothing more in that alcove than a sack of brown paper."

"Indeed. The paper was the costume used by Mr Lionel Watting to make it appear that the mummy had stolen the Sceptre. It was composed of paper cut into strips and dyed to resemble burial wrappings, probably with tea. I noticed that it was spattered with a small amount of blood, hence the significance of the

193

bandage that we have seen. Probably Watting cut himself, either on the sceptre or some other sharp object, during the theft. I recognised the typeface used by *The Times* at once, and Mr Watting's confirmation, together with his knowledge of Egyptology and of the museum, was immediately suggestive since Mr Thomas Glowry, as a cripple and the only other possible thief besides our client, is clearly incapable of such acts. Mr Watting, having entered the building undetected, hid in the alcove until he was certain that only Mr Pindler remained, before putting on the makeshift costume and stealing the Sceptre. He was well acquainted with Mr Pindler's condition of nervous weakness, and knew that this would result in a fainting spell long before he drew near enough to determine the true nature of the apparition before him. Mr Watting then rid himself of his disguise in the alcove, before leaving the building unseen. It seems likely that he also knew of Mr Pindler's past crime that was certain to cause him to be blamed for the theft."

"But what was the purpose of the robbery? Does Mr Watting intend to keep the Sceptre for his own satisfaction?"

"I think not, but for confirmation I must make a few calls after breakfast tomorrow, and then perhaps a visit to Mycroft."

#

I saw that Holmes had begun his calls early, for Mrs Hudson had already cleared away the remains of his breakfast as I entered our sitting room. The locum who had temporarily assumed the practice of my colleague, Doctor Mayfield, had struck me as rather inexperienced so, in Holmes' absence, I seized the opportunity to visit his surgery to conduct a check on the fellow. I was pleased to see that he had managed extraordinarily well, and I returned to Baker Street earlier than I had anticipated.

I had hardly had time to settle myself in an armchair, much less to light my pipe or call to Mrs Hudson for tea, before the front door slammed and Holmes' footsteps rang heavily on the stairs. He burst into the room, and quickly shed his hat and coat.

"I perceive that you have visited the surgery of one of your friends, Watson. I hope all was well there."

I rose, surprised by this unexpected observation. "Is there nothing that can be hidden from you, Holmes?"

"Many things, I am sure, but nothing as simple as the traces of mud on the side of your boots and the borrowed medical journal bearing today's date that you have left sticking out of your bag. I know that no such publication was delivered here this morning."

"You never cease to amaze me," I scowled. "Was your own morning successful?"

He lowered himself into one of the other chairs. "Extremely so. I have spoken to several of my underworld acquaintances, and met briefly with brother Mycroft in the Strangers Room at the Diogenes Club. Everything is as I suspected and," he consulted his pocket-watch, "as it is scarcely past the hour of three o'clock I see no reason why this affair cannot be brought to its conclusion this very day. Assuming, old fellow, that you are willing to accompany me after your earlier exertions."

The second journey to Lord Galtacre's estate seemed shorter than before. Mr Watting's residence appeared unoccupied as we passed it on our way along the gravel drive to the imposing Tudor manor house that stood ahead.

An elderly butler answered Holmes' rapping on the iron-studded front door. At the sight of us he announced immediately that his master was not at home, whereupon my friend wrote 'The Sceptre of Anubis' on a scrap of paper and asked the man to deliver it. A few minutes later we found ourselves in a drawing-room bedecked with landscapes and portraits on every wall, while Roman and Egyptian artefacts stood on marble plinths among the furniture.

For the first few moments we were alone, then the door was flung back and a short man in hunting clothes strode in. His anger was immediately apparent, the eyes that stared from above the full beard that hid much of his face were filled with fury.

"What is the meaning of this intrusion? Who dares to suggest that I have stolen this bauble? Who are you?"

Holmes answered in a mild, even tone. "My name is Sherlock Holmes, Lord Galtacre. I am, as you may know, a consulting detective. I have been given the task of retrieving the Sceptre of Anubis but have not, as yet, accused anyone of its theft. It has come to my notice however, that Mr Lionel Watting who you employ has obtained many works of art and historical significance on your behalf, sometimes resorting to crime to do so." He glanced around the room. "I wonder, how many of these excellent examples are copies, and how many are originals long since thought to have disappeared after theft. I do not think it will be long before the truth is extracted from Mr Watting during a police interview, and the resulting scandal will swiftly follow. I am here to advise you to return the Sceptre, and distance yourself from his fate."

The effect of Holmes' words on Lord Galtacre was increasingly evident. His face had turned a deeper red and his expression hardened with anger. When he spoke, the words came out with much effort, as from one who has difficulty breathing.

"How dare you, sir! By God, I will not tolerate this!" He raised the riding crop that was clenched in his right hand, holding it as if to strike my friend a heavy blow.

196

"I would strongly advise against that, your Lordship," Holmes said calmly. "Such an act would do nothing but make matters worse."

"Get out of my house, before I have you thrown out!"

"We are glad to acquiesce, but I should perhaps mention that the official force, as well as myself, are aware of your past dealings with professional art thieves and the circumstances of your dismissal from your club. The outcome of all this is entirely in your own hands."

"Leave my house immediately!"

"Goodbye, your Lordship."

#

Holmes bid the driver of the hansom that we had procured during our walk towards Harrow to stop and wait for us, while he despatched a telegram to Lestrade.

"I have told the inspector that he can safely arrest Mr Watting," he told me on resuming his seat. "Enough evidence was provided by my underworld acquaintances to establish that the man has used his knowledge to organise thefts before now. It would be interesting to find out how many discoveries have disappeared from the store room of the British Museum, before they could be catalogued."

"He has acted as an agent, in that respect, for Lord Galtacre before?"

"So Mycroft assures me. Apparently his Lordship is quite notorious, an obsessive collector of culture. He is singularly ruthless in his methods, often offering large sums to the owners of artefacts that he wishes to make his own. On several occasions, a refusal to sell has been followed by the theft of the icon concerned soon after. It was one such incident, although his responsibility was never proven, that resulted in him losing his membership of his Pall Mall club."

"They wished to avoid any connection with a possible scandal," I said as the driver brought the horse to a halt near our lodgings.

"Precisely. Lord Galtacre is not popular among his peers."

#

We heard nothing more of the affair for three days. Mrs Hudson had barely cleared away the remains of our breakfasts when she reappeared bearing two telegrams for Holmes.

"Ah, yes," my friend said as he identified the senders. "everything has turned out exactly as I hoped, Watson."

"I am glad to hear it."

Holmes dropped the torn envelopes onto the unlit kindling in the fireplace. "The first message is from Lestrade. He has looked into Mr Watting's activities as I suggested, and found ample evidence for an arrest. Apparently Lord Galtacre's agent did not cover his tracks well, doubtlessly in the belief that his employer's position made the effort unnecessary. As for his Lordship, he embarked on a long sea voyage, but when Lestrade's men visited his residence they found not a single work of art."

"He must have disposed of his collection rather quickly."

"I would imagine he had made advance preparations, in case his methods of acquisition ever came to light. Not that it matters now, for Lestrade tells us of a report received from the French police. It seems that Lord Galtacre's first stop was the port of

Marseilles, which is the hunting-ground of much of the local criminal classes. Possibly his prosperous appearance caused the attack upon his person, for he was certainly robbed of all that he carried. He did not survive, however."

I leaned forward in my chair. "What of the second telegram, Holmes?"

"That is from our former client, Mr Randolph Pindler. He thanks us for restoring the faith of his employer, Mr Glowry, in him, and for the increased salary he has received by way of apology. He also states, and this is especially satisfying, that a plain wooden box was delivered anonymously to the British Museum yesterday. It contained, among much careful packing, the missing Sceptre of Anubis."

"A most satisfactory conclusion to your investigation." I agreed.

Holmes reached for his clay pipe and proceeded to fill it from the Persian slipper. "That being certain, old fellow, it occurs to me that it has been some little while since we have allowed ourselves dinner at Simpsons. What do you say to giving Mrs Hudson the evening to herself, while we again sample their cuisine?"